No Quarter
Shifter Chronicles
Book 3

ANITA COX

Printed in the United States of America.

Visit us on line at www.SynPublishing.com

ISBN:
1-942632-22-3
ISBN-13: 978-1-942632-22-1

DEDICATION

To my family, who put up with countless hours of my face behind the laptop. To Dawn H. for always keeping me on my toes and to Crystal and Ella for sticking with me

And always to my fans. I thank you for sticking with me through the years and all of the kind words.

Table of Contents

ANITA COX

ONE

Nala Baker took her job as the first female Alpha seriously. A responsibility which required she be sharp physically as well as mentally. She bent at the waist, touching her toes, feeling her muscles stretching. After standing straight, she grabbed the front of her ankle and stretched her leg behind her, then repeated with her other leg before she set off down the trail, first at a slow jog.

The early morning light peered through the trees, shooting golden beams on the path before her. The cool morning air brushed against her face, cooling her body which heated up quickly during runs. Morning dew sparkled in the light, causing her face to twitch into a smile. The forest was waking. The sweet earthy aroma amplified by the dew was sweet in her nose.

It was only a matter of time before some male showed up and challenged her for her spot. It could be a member of her own pack. When they did, they'd pay for that mistake. She swore the day she took the life of her last abusive male Alpha, she'd never have a man in charge of her life again. She'd die first.

As each foot took its turn pounding against the forest floor, her heart thundered in her chest. Her thighs began to burn as she picked up the pace. She claimed the forest in her mind, obsessed over every small detail of pack business. The farmers' production began to increase with a few suggestions by Tiffany, a pack member who was attending McGovern University, the first university exclusively for supernatural students.

Things were going well. Her arranged marriage to Colin was still stiff. They'd held hands, exchanged pleasantries and had even taken to quick pecks on the cheek when greeting or departing each other. They'd yet to take their relationship any further. It was an internal struggle for them both. Colin, still grieving his late wife and child, and Nala, a victim of heinous acts of her former Alpha hadn't been ready to consummate the relationship.

But she wanted more than a friendly business arrangement. Though she'd never admit it to anyone else, she mourned that special bond she'd never had. She wanted to enjoy sex again. She'd have to be vulnerable to her mate, yet seem completely invulnerable to everyone else. That was a riddle she'd yet to solve.

Reaching her favorite tree, with a nice level branch, she leaped up and grabbed it with both hands. She pulled herself up, lifting her chin above the branch, then lowering herself until her arms were fully extended. She repeated the movement twenty-four more times, reveling in the burn that rippled through her biceps and shoulders before she'd drop back to the ground and commence her run.

Five more minutes and she'd reach the main house. Slowing her pace slightly, she considered Jake. Colin's half-brother and look-alike had been selected as her Beta. It was a less than popular decision for the women, who came with her from the Scottsboro pack, but she had to blend the two packs together and Jake was a nice bridge between the old regime and the new. He was also effective and loyal, two qualities Nala held in high regard.

She finally reached the main house and stopped, taking a moment to gain her composure before entering the house, which was always buzzing with Lycans first thing in the morning. Closing her eyes, she tilted her face toward the sun, reveling in the warmth of the rays licking at her skin.

"I, uh, brought you a glass of water."

She opened her eyes and watched as Colin approached holding a glass of water in his hand. She found him handsome the first time they'd met. When he was nervous, he'd trip on his tongue or run his fingers through his thick wavy blond locks.

"That was thoughtful. Thank you." With a smile she took the glass out of his hand and took a long drink, thankful to have the cool water running down her throat, which was hot and dry from her run. He always seemed to attempt to take care of her in some manner, just like bringing her a glass of water after her morning run.

"Breakfast is almost ready." He stared at her for two seconds more than was comfortable before turning on his heel and heading back into the house.

Would the awkwardness ever go away?

Releasing a breath she hadn't realized she was holding, she followed him into the house. Maybe she should make the first move. Maybe she should plan an intimate dinner. Maybe...she didn't know what the hell she was doing.

She took her usual seat at the head of the table with Colin, with his golden hair, blue eyes and dark skin sitting to her right. Jake sat to her left. The two men often exchanged uncomfortable glances with each other and while it ate at Nala, not knowing what was behind the exchange, she couldn't bring herself to ask her mate if there was a problem. Maybe it was because Colin was the former Alpha of the Belfast pack and his current position as her advisor was in conflict with her having a Beta whose job it was to be her right hand man. Perhaps it was sibling rivalry. Whatever it was made her squirm in her chair. The tension was nearly palpable.

She sipped at her coffee as she considered them. After settling on turning a blind eye, she cut into her Country Fried Steak, appreciating the wonderful food she enjoyed instead of the slop she'd been fed in the not-so-distant past. Dipping a biscuit into the gravy she glanced around and watched her pack mates as they smiled and conversed over breakfast. The only place there didn't seem to be harmony was her little corner of the table, with the mate she'd yet to bond and his half-brother.

Wendy Baker, Colin's sister, had requested the Belfast pack to take the little people in. They needed protection so -they didn't have to live like rodents and in return, they would work around the pack contributing in any way they could. It seemed like a fair arrangement. Tiny houses were built among the Lycan houses. Two dozen little homes butted up to larger ones that offered protection from the elements.

In return, farmers had help milking cows, feeding chickens, and collecting eggs. The Gnomes had an enormous garden they tended with herbs and vegetables that they distributed among the pack. Some of them had taken to child care, or HVAC work, running or repairing duct work in what would be cramped attic space to a Lycan. Two of the Gnomes were experts and locating, cutting and polishing jewels and had taken to selling extravagant jewelry, mostly to the Vampires, who were fond of such baubles. Though Nala had been wary of taking on what she thought would be an extra responsibility, so far the relationship had been quite symbiotic.

Zoltar, Wendy's new mate and the Centaur King, and his men had begun manufacturing small automobiles for the Gnomes so that they could get around more easily. Little jeep-like vehicles with fat tires to maneuver among rocks and branches carried the little people all over the property.

"I was thinking," she started, in an effort to break the tension, "maybe we can put some crushed stone paths down for the Gnomes' cars. I know their little cars get them around but it has to be a bumpy ride around this terrain."

Jake pulled out a small pad of paper he kept in his front pocket and jotted it down. "I'll get some quotes." He tucked the paper back into the pocket and continued eating.

It took every ounce of control for her not to roll her eyes. "Colin, I was thinking about going into town today. Would you care to join me?" She placed her fork on her plate and folded her hands in her lap. When she turned to him she found him beaming at her, his smile wide.

"I'd like that very much."

Her heart fluttered. She returned his smile. "By the time I'm cleaned up and finish some paperwork, it'll be nearly lunch. Maybe we can have lunch in town?"

He slid his hand across the table and placed his hand on hers, giving a gentle squeeze. "That sounds perfect." Scooting back from the table, he dropped his napkin on his chair and left the dining room.

She watched the back of him as he left, his head held a little higher than when he brought her the water. He even seemed to have a bit of a spring in his step.

Returning her focus back to the table, she caught the end of Jake rolling his eyes.

"Something on your mind?" She crossed her arms over her chest and narrowed her eyes.

"Not a thing." He jerked his chair back and tossed his fork down on his plate before making his own quick departure.

Men.

"Thank you for the breakfast, Trace." She smiled at Tracy, her most trusted female companion and who she'd intended to be her Beta before coming to the Belfast pack. Tracy had handled it well, insisting on her desire for peace being greater than any need for position. She now managed the house, which was a far cry from Beta duties. She hated seeing her friend stuck in a traditional domestic role, but Tracy never complained, be it pride, or the appreciation of a domestic role rather than a lifetime in captivity.

After excusing herself she made her way to room. She kicked off her shoes and walked into the bathroom, peeling off her clothes. She turned on the shower and stepped in, closing her eyes as the water poured over her. She had to think of a reason to go into town. It was a spur of the moment decision to spend some time with her mate. But now, she needed an excuse. What would they do once they arrived? Where, exactly, would they go?

She tried to concoct a plan as she lathered her hair with soap. Nothing came to mind at first. Jake took care of ordering supplies. Tracy had always made sure they were well stocked with feminine products. She could use some clothes. She hadn't come with much and what little she had was wearing thin. The Alpha shouldn't dress like a bum, but would Colin be bored out of his mind shopping for clothes?

Of course he would, he was a man.

She sighed. It was the only excuse she could devise.

After a quick conditioning of her hair and a good scrub she was rinsed and drying off.

"Uh, Nala?" Colin called through the door.

Her heart jumped into her throat. He hadn't seen her naked yet and this was not how she wanted it to go. "I'll be out in a moment." She called out, throwing her robe on and cinching it closed.

"Oh, hi." He looked away when she opened the door. "I just…uh…was wondering…Um…You didn't say what we were doing in town. Do I need to get the truck ready?"

She felt a smirk forming on her face as she tried to hide her amusement. "Colin?"

He looked at her. "I don't want you to think, you know, that I was trying to catch you in the shower or anything. I came to get my wallet and heard you in there."

She let go of a chuckle. "It's okay. We don't need the truck. I actually need some clothes and we always have everyone around here watching us so closely. I thought it might be nice for us to spend some time together while not being under a microscope. I hope clothes shopping won't be too much of a drag for you."

Holding his chin a little higher, he said, "I happen to have excellent taste in women's apparel. I was considering getting a new pair of heels myself."

She nearly gasped when he winked at her. He'd only done it a few times before. He'd always seemed to flirt with her when she least expected it, but never really when she did.

"Well, not in red. It would clash with your eyes."

His throaty laugh made her heart ache. He really needed to laugh more. When he smiled it made his eyes squint a little at the sides. He had a sweet boyish look to him when he laughed. It was endearing and very rare, at least in her experience.

Glancing down at his feet, he kicked at the floor. "Okay then. I'll just go. See you in a bit." Before she could do or say anything else, he made a quick exit.

She walked over to the bed and sat on the edge. Her heat was coming soon and she certainly didn't want their first time to be during a heat. With a heavy heart she walked into her closet to dressed, her eyes falling to the note she found that morning hidden under her coffee cup. It's pasted lettering warning her; *enjoy your power while you can female alpha…it's about to end!*

.

TWO

Nala finished the paperwork on the newest pack arrival, a new pup. The FOSE, or Federation of Supernatural Entities, had created a registry to track and manage the supernaturals so there wouldn't be any more lost souls among them. It was a great idea, but it came with forms she had to fill out on her computer. Then the pack Alpha and the pack doctor both had to scan their thumb print along with the baby's foot.

She put the registry number into the scanner and headed downstairs. She looked around until she found Tracy folding laundry. The woman's hair was so bright red it reminded Nala of fire. "Want to take a walk with me? I have to go register the new pup before going into town with Colin."

Tracy nodded and tossed the last towel into the basket. "Absolutely."

Neither of them spoke a word until they were outside and away from the others. Even though the two packs had merged, they still felt a little on the outside and felt more comfortable speaking alone.

"Want to tell me what's eating you?" Tracy asked as she nudged Nala with her shoulder.

She should have confided in her mate…or her Beta. But the tension between them would only worsen if she threw concern in the mix. "There was a note left in my room."

Tracy glanced at her before turning her attention back to the path. "A note?"

After a deep breath, she nodded. "The threatening kind."

"Well I'm not surprised. We figured this would happen. Lycan men don't like women in charge. What does Colin say?" Tracy tucked her hands in her pockets as their pace slowed to a stroll.

"I haven't told him yet. It could be nothing. Right? Just a jealous youngster who thought they were in line for the throne?" She knew that wasn't the case. Her worst case scenario was about to unfold.

A small grin spread across her friend's lips. Was that her friend finding solace that she still trusted her more than her own mate or her second in command?

Tracy tossed her hair over her shoulder. "Anything else bothering you?"

Oh God yes…Do I tell her? "My heat is coming. Two weeks tops, if I'm lucky." Her face burned hot, embarrassed about the personal nature of her problem. "Emotionally, I'm not sure I'm ready."

"For pups?" Tracy furrowed her brow.

Nala looked at her fiery red hair bounce and sway as she walked. "Oh, no. Not…well, no not yet. I mean to be intimate."

"Are you fucking mental?" Tracy stopped walking. She crossed her arms over her chest.

She turned to face her. "That's not the supportive speech I was expecting from *you* of all people."

"Nala! Do you realize you're the only member form our old pack to even have a date much less a mate. They all tiptoe around us like we're lepers. Hell, we'd all like to have a little consensual sex now that we're able. And you have a hot mate and you *don't* want to have sex with him?"

Her shoulders fell. "We haven't...you don't understand. We haven't gotten there yet."

"Why the hell not?"

She felt her jaw fall slack. "What do you mean? Because of what we went through. Because, he's been in mourning. Because we're both a hot mess. Because it was an arranged marriage." Her friend's reaction was a betrayal. She wanted comfort. She wanted understanding. Hell, even some advice would help. Tracy's shock and seeming jealousy didn't bode well.

"Nala, honey... we're all a mess. Us—them, we just have to move forward. If we don't, Jagger wins. He destroyed us. We can't let that happen. What happened to the kick-ass-take-charge Alpha we all adore? Because this," she wagged her finger up and down toward Nala, "this is lame. This is weak. It's *your* sex life. It's *your* marriage. Take charge of it." After shaking her head, she put her hands on her hips. "I followed you into battle. I watched two of my sisters get murdered and *still* followed you into battle. If you can't take charge of your own life, how are you supposed to take charge of the rest *of us?*" Her voice pitched at the end, accentuating her level of exacerbation.

Feeling her nails digging into her palms, she measured up her closest confidant. Her words may have been cold, but that's why she adored Tracy—the woman never held back. She always said exactly what she was thinking.

"It's possible I forgot how to have a healthy relationship." After a large sigh, she stomped off toward the doctor's quarters. "I'll figure it out. Thanks for the pep talk."

"Anytime!" Tracy yelled out from behind her.

If she didn't feel pathetic before her little chat, she certainly did after. The thought of her pack sisters' envy hadn't crossed her mind.

Maryann, the doctor, greeted her at the door. "So nice to see you, Nala."

She forced a smile on her face, though she suspected Maryann could sense her tension. "Came to greet our newest arrival."

"Right this way," she held her arm out toward the hall.

Nala stepped in then allowed her to lead. The pack's medical building was no bigger than a good sized doctor's office with two birthing suites, a triage room and one surgical area, which was rarely used. When she entered the birthing suite she found two weepy parents cooing over their new bundle of joy. "Congratulations. He's a fine young specimen."

Reaching into the blanket to find the infant's foot she stared at the little toes that peeked out. They were tiny, no bigger than pencil erasers. She fought the urge to smooch on the top of the chubby little foot. With the softest of pressure she pushed the scanner against the tiny little foot and then tucked it back into the blanket.

The parents thanked her. She stood for a moment as she absorbed the love in the room. The mother, tired from childbirth didn't let that slow down her affection toward her new little package. The father beamed at them both with alligator tears threatening to spill over his cheeks. The squeezing sensation in her chest made it harder to breathe.

She tried to imagine herself in that moment, staring down at her own pup with the same loving adoration. It seemed like a far off fairy tale she may never experience. Hell, she couldn't even bring herself to mate with her own husband.

Michelle, a fellow Scottsboro pack member had fed her milk thistle for so long, trying to delay her heats so Jagger would not force a mating on her, that she'd gone three years without one. Even in those three years, she hadn't forgotten how intense the desire was. But she was feeling that familiar edge that comes before a heat and knew it was approaching.

She was desperate for that burning physical desire to breed to be far from her first time making love with her mate. She wanted the romance, more than she was willing to admit, but had kept Colin at arm's length.

Backing out of the room, she quickly made her way out of the building and on the path toward the main house. Without haste, she made her way through the house, so as not to interact with anyone, fearful that her emotions would get the best of her. After plugging the scanner into her computer, she grabbed her bag and headed out to the parking lot to meet with Colin.

As her feet crunched against the gravel parking area, she tried to force her shoulders to relax. Colin was leaning against a Honda Civic, staring off into the woods. His gaze changed, moving to the direction of her approach. He pushed his weight off the car and opened the passenger door.

"Ready for our date?" His eyes turned to slits as he smiled.

"Thank you, Colin." He was always a gentleman, a quality she had a difficult time becoming accustomed to. She took a deep breath after he closed her door. *Relax. Stay calm. You're already married.*

He climbed in and started the car. "Are you ready for lunch?"

She shrugged. "Not yet, really. But I am ready to get out of here for a while."

Driving the car down the winding drive he didn't say much until they had hit the main road. "You know, we can hit a few shops before we grab lunch. There's a really decent Bistro in town."

"That sounds great. As far as the clothes shopping goes, I don't need anything fancy, just some day to day items." She cleared her throat. "You know, jeans, shorts, shirts…things like that. I don't really know the stores around here."

Glancing quickly toward her, then away, he bobbed his head. "You strike me as someone who would appreciate Kohl's or something along those lines."

She felt her left brow shoot toward her hairline. "What

does that mean, exactly?"

"It means you don't want to look too fancy. You dress so you can defend yourself at all times. Shoes, boots, jeans…those are your staple items. I don't think we need a Macy's for that." His right eyebrow lifted toward his hairline. "Though I'd be lying if I said I wasn't eager to see you dressed up for a party."

She laughed and wagged her finger at him. "You have. We've been together for two weddings, one of them our own."

Shrugging, he gave a soft chuckle. "Like I said, I'm eager to see you dressed up for a party. You look ravishing in a dress."

His compliment caused heat to graze her cheeks. He found her ravishing…that was a great sign.

The couple made small talk about parties until they reached the store. After locking the car, he reached in his pocket and answered his cell phone. Whatever had been said had caused him to stop walking.

"Is everything okay?"

She watched as his smile faded and his brows creased together.

"But you want to talk in person? What's happened?" He was rubbing his forehead, something he often did when stressed. "Wendy, I'm your brother, that's why. I don't understand why you have to see me in person if it's not…" He stopped speaking, took a deep breath, and let it out. He pulled the phone away from his face. "Would you like to accompany me to the school to have dinner with my sister tonight?"

She gave him an affirmative nod. Whatever was going on with his sister had him stressed. She could feel it rolling off of him. So she would most certainly go with him to have a meal and get to the bottom of things. Besides, there was very little going on in Belfast.

"See you at six." He shoved the phone back in his pocket. "I'm very sorry about the interruption."

They began walking toward the store once again. "Something up with your sister?"

"Yes, and of course she's being cryptic and won't tell me anything over the phone but still expects me not to worry. How am I *not* supposed to worry? It isn't like she calls me regularly." Shaking his head, he opened the door for her.

"Well, Colin, it's our job as women to drive you barking mad." She forced a smile and entered the store.

He hadn't misled her. She discovered he actually had very good taste in women's clothing, even casual wear. When a pair of pants didn't fit her well, he never made mention of them being unflattering or making her rear look too big. Instead, he would offer something such as, 'those aren't good enough for you,' or, 'try these on.' Everything else earned compliments. It had been quite the ego boost. After an hour of picking out jeans that complimented her shape while affording her full range of motion, flattering shorts and tops, they were paying for her purchase.

When they arrived at the bistro, Nala addressed the hostess right away. "Can we sit off to the side," she paused, "for a little privacy?" If she were going to have a serious discussion with her mate, she didn't want the world to be privy to it.

"Certainly. Right this way." She slid her fingers under two menus and scooped them up, then led them to the far side of the restaurant, took their drink orders, and scurried away.

As soon as she was out of ear shot, Colin leaned in on his elbows. "Tired of having everyone hear and see everything we do and say?"

His baby blue button down shirt complimented his blue eyes and tanned skin. The brilliant white teeth glistened at her. "Yes, well, if we're ever going to get privacy outside of the bedroom, this might be the only way."

"I have to say," he said while shaking out his napkin, "I don't mind whisking you away."

The waitress returned with their beverages and took

their food orders.

"Okay, now that we're alone…" she took a deep breath, "there's something rather…uncomfortable we need to discuss." She tried to find the courage, the right words, so that it didn't sound like a business arrangement. After years living under Jagger's regime, she'd grown quite adapt to not displaying fear and panic. She used every skill she had to remain still and calm while her insides felt like they were melting.

"Well this sounds interesting. Continue." His smile appeared to be forced, possibly for her benefit. He took a slow sip of his tea while playfully wagging his brows. She didn't mind. The fact that he tried to keep it light actually made her feel a bit better.

"We have both been taking things…very slow—out of respect for each other mostly. We were both trying to heal from very different but equally horrifying ordeals." Smoothing her hands on her pants she forced herself to look up at him.

The smile was gone and a serious look now took residence on his face. He was nearly expressionless with his mouth open slightly and his eyes open and focused. Did she scare him already?

"Go on," he croaked.

Plotting Jagger's demise was a cakewalk next to attempting to discuss her love life with her husband. She took a deep breath and let it out, then sipped at her soda, buying her time to find the courage. She closed her eyes tight and finally, as she opened her eyes, released the words. "My heat is coming and very soon."

"I see." His hands slid off the table and disappeared below the surface.

Punching him in the throat wouldn't help him say any more than 'I see' but the thought had crossed her mind. *Say something!*

"We've yet to get to that, uh, aspect. But I'd rather it not be during a heat. That's not how I want to—"

He held his hand up, interrupting her. "I know this is uncomfortable, and not to make it worse, but I want to remind you that I've been mated before. I am familiar with what you're about to go through and how difficult it can be. Anything I can do to help. I mean," His face turned as red as a cherry tomato, "I mean, if you want me out of the room until you've recovered or something... or privacy...or, oh man, anything. I'm sorry. I, uh, I mean, uh."

She lifted her head.

He looked down—a sign of submission by a Lycan.

She felt her eyes widen in surprise.

"Colin, look at me, please." When his eyes met hers, she smiled. "What I'm saying is I would like us to get there *before* it happens. I mean to say I'm ready to try to move forward, but I don't have the slightest idea where you are with this because...well because we don't really talk much, not about anything personal." As embarrassed as she was to discuss the matter, and as nervous as she had been, relief washed over her now that the words had finally come out. "The problem is we haven't had much time to act like an actual couple because we've been so focused on giving each other space. And now, with my heat coming, we don't have much time to get there beforehand. I'm tired of things just happening to me. Life has just happened to me. Life stopped happening when I defeated Jagger. I'd like to continue taking control, but this isn't just me, here. This involves you too."

She noticed his eyes shift, looking behind her. The waitress was coming and the discussion took a brief halt while their lunch was delivered. Even though the food was in front of them, neither took a bite.

His gazed fixed on hers as she waited for him to speak.

"Dinner tonight with my sister would be a nice start. And when we retire for the evening, we can do things a little differently. We can start turning in a little earlier, so we can talk privately in our room. We can stop avoiding each other quite so much. But there is one sure fire way for us to feel what we both so desperately want to feel."

She gulped, knowing exactly to what he referred. "I'm not sure bonding is a great idea."

His shoulders slumped. "Why not?"

Scooting her plate to the side, she placed her elbows on the table and folded her hands, leaning forward, nearly whispering. "Has it occurred to you it is only a matter of time before someone challenges me for my position?"

The realization of her situation had to have hit him, because his mouth fell open. "It'll be no quarter."

She gave one short but firm bob of her chin. "And you'll suffer that loss all over again. You'll lose your second bonded mate. I can't do that to you, Colin. We may not yet be in love, but I respect you too much to hurt you that way."

The silence between them lingered as he stared at her. He broke his gaze and picked up his sandwich. "Don't you think that's my risk to take?"

It hadn't occurred to her decision would take away his choice. "I hadn't considered it. But in all fairness we haven't really had any discussions about us at all. As a matter of fact, we've hardly had any discussions about anything." She folded her hands and let them rest in her lap. If there wasn't already anxiety over simply having the discussion, her impending heat and the strange nature of their union, she now was filled with anxiety, concerned she'd insulted him. Worse yet, she'd been famished when they reached the restaurant and now her stomach was in such knots her sandwich was less than appealing.

"I have to admit, it is a concern." He finally spoke. "I'm not sure I could survive it a second time. It is just one thing to consider. We were thrown together with so much baggage it might take a life time to sift through it all. It's one way we can be certain to break through these barriers, to be sure we're not pushing the other too quickly." He took a deep breath and let it out. "Either way, let's table it for now. You need to eat."

She looked down at the slice of wheat bread resting on

the top of her sandwich. It looked less appealing than it had when it arrived. Still, she forced herself to take a bite. The rest of lunch was rather quiet and uncomfortable. She managed to choke down half her meal before she gave up.

As he drove them back to the Belfast pack's territory, she gazed out the window. Every single decision she made now had a consequence. As Alpha of a pack, they were all subject to the consequences of her decisions. On a personal level, if she did bond with Colin to break through the barriers they'd both built, and was then killed in a fight to the death for her Alpha position, he'd suffer a horrible injustice of nature once again. If she didn't bond with him, they may never connect the way a Lycan couple should. This left her with nothing more than a feeling of dread.

When they parked the car, she quickly thanked him for the lunch and hurried up to her room to put her things away. In order to make dinner with Wendy, Colin's sister, on time, she'd have to quickly change, check her messages and be ready to leave.

She was fond of Wendy but had requested she leave and join the new school. Dinner would at least sate her curiosity regarding Wendy's transition. Standing in her closet, she decided on one of the few pant suits she had and stripped down to her underwear and bra, quickly pulling on the tan pants. Colin had always dressed well and it *was* a dinner. His mate shouldn't sport jeans and a tank top while accompanying him to a family meeting. Tossing the jacket and flats on the bed as she crossed the room to the bathroom, she worked quickly to get her long dark hair into a French twist and applied a little mascara.

"How do you do that?" Colin asked from the bedroom, staring in at her as she smoothed a tinted lip balm across her bottom lip.

"Do what?"

"Transform, that's what. You look like a different woman, entirely." He shook his head. "This is how I saw you the very first time. I distinctly remember my jaw hitting the floor."

She felt the smile spreading across her face. "All I remember was you could hardly put two words together."

He leaned his forearm against the door jamb. "Well yeah, I was speechless. You truly are a vision, Nala. Don't think for one moment I don't find you absolutely stunning just because our union was arranged." He winked before abruptly turning and walking into his own large closet.

And there it was. He was flirting again. The ride home was quiet. Why didn't he choose then to flirt? Why not over lunch? Why now after a long awkward drive home? He left her standing, speechless, at the bathroom mirror.

"Because we spend too much time protecting ourselves. We don't notice it all of the time." Her wolf, which had been entirely too absent finally spoke to her. *"We must learn to relax. He is a good wolf."*

It was now or never. He had flirted, complimented, and assured her of his physical attraction. After a deep, cleansing breath, she put her head forward and marched into his closet.

He was tucking in his dress shirt when he froze, surprised to see her in his space. She took three slow steps closing the distance between them. Easing her hand up, she placed her palm on his cheek and leaned in, hopeful. He didn't miss his cue, closing the one solitary inch between them, locking their lips in their first kiss. It was brief and respectful…tender, yet full of need.

Her heart raced and she wasn't sure if it were nerves or butterflies tying her stomach into knots.

"Thank you for the compliment. It feels really nice." She leaned back on her heels easing back from him, releasing his face. "I'm looking forward to dinner."

Maybe the ride to the school would be more pleasant than the ride home from shopping. She gave him a quick smile before hurrying out of the closet to let him finish dressing. Silently, she chastised herself for not paying more attention, of noting his reaction. It wasn't easy when she was so focused on being brave enough to take the first important step.

Her head snapped at a tiny knock on their bedroom door. She began walking toward it to answer when Colin rushed in front of her. "No you don't!" When he opened the door, Thomas one of the Gnomes stood holding a small black box in his hand.

"Mr. Baker, here is your order. I do hope they are to your liking." He lifted the box up and Colin scooped it out of his hand.

"I'm sure it's perfect, Thomas. Thank you."

"Mrs. Baker," the tiny man bobbed his head, "have a great evening."

"What was that about?" she asked as he shut the door.

He closed the distance between them and held the black box in his palm, which was stretched out toward her. "A gift for my wife."

Her mouth fell slack and her heart throbbed in her chest. He'd procured a gift for her. She could not remember the last time anyone gave her a gift, especially for no reason. She lifted the small box from his hand and opened it, finding two pink garnet earrings, hand carved by the Gnomes. A matching garnet studded bracelet rested at the bottom.

"Colin!" she gasped holding the box away from her. "This is too much."

With gentle pressure, and a smile plastered on his face, he pushed it back toward her. "No. It isn't. You are Alpha of this pack. You are my mate. It's a simple gift I would love to see you wear to dinner tonight." He stepped closer and ran his hand along her arm. "And that's nickel, due to your strong aversion to silver."

At a loss for words, she bravely stepped in and wrapped her arms around him. She could feel his warm arms wrapping around her ribs, then shoulders, pulling her into him. When at last she finally released him, she saw that familiar smirk in his eyes.

"I expected the kiss to happen *after* the jewelry." He

chuckled and tucked his hands in the pockets of his slacks, his eyes pointed at the floor.

"Seems we're both full of surprises." She placed the box on the bureau near her and put the jewelry on. When she was finished, she turned to look in the mirror. The pink garnet looked nice against her dark skin. "Thank you very much."

* * * *

The ride to the school had, indeed, been more relaxed than the ride home from shopping. They chatted about small things, getting to know each other's taste in everything from music to adult beverages. It felt nice to her, having someone become familiar. Colin had scooped her hand in his and held it during the ride. His warmth oozed into her, relaxing her tension.

As they drove down the long lane toward the school Nala felt her eyes bulge. The center of the building looked like a large castle. The East and West wings were large and rectangular in shape, continuing the same stone work as the castle.

"Wow, that's huge! I had no idea the school was so grand." Her eyes darted around, trying to take in every little detail.

He squeezed her hand. "From what I've heard the inside is even more spectacular." After parking in the rear of the school they were approached my two Centaurs.

"Hello, you must be Colin and Nala Baker," one of them said.

"Yes, and you are?" Nala extended her hand.

He leaned over and shook her hand. "My name is Prometheus. This is Theron. We are to escort you to Wendy's door since it's easy to get lost in the school your first time." Led by two Centaurs thru the building, they walked into a great hall. Her gaze danced from side hall to stairs, to little Gnomes zipping around in their cars. Each hall had been marked at the entrance with carved numbers and letters.

"Glad I chose flats," she whispered.

Theron looked over his shoulder. "This is the West wing. We will be there in a moment."

They turned left down another corridor.

"This is your sister's door. We'll leave you now." The Centaurs turned and left them standing.

After a nervous glance at her, Colin knocked.

"Grace?" The color had drained form Colin's face as the door opened. "Where's Wendy?"

Grace smiled and pulled him in through the door. "Oh, I'm fine. How are you, Colin? It's good to see you." She rolled her eyes. "Hello, Nala. How are you?"

"I'm good, Grace. It's nice to see you again." She gave a brief respectful nod to her Queen.

Roman sat on the sofa, looking as if he were avoiding eye contact with Colin. She picked up on it right away, but thought a distraction would serve them well. "Look at the beautiful jewelry Colin just gave me. Isn't it nice?"

Grace admired the jewelry, stepping between Colin and his view of his former Beta, playfully winking at her. The glint in her eye spoke of good news, though Nala couldn't understand the subterfuge.

"Wendy will be out in a minute. Dinner is nearly ready. If you'd like to move to the dining room." A man stood with golden hair and bronzed skin atop bulging muscles which were barely contained in his white shirt. Nala recognized him as Zoltar, the Centaur King.

"How often do you get a Centaur King cooking for you?" Nala joked, elbowing Colin in the ribs. She had a feeling she knew what was about to take place. Colin's mood might change for the worse.

"Scotch?" Grace asked, wagging a decanter in her hand.

Colin only bobbed his head as he looked back and forth between Zoltar and Roman.

"Zoltar has some wine if you'd prefer that over scotch,

Nala." Grace smiled at her. "He really has a knack for picking wine too."

A compliment to the Centaur King…as if he needed one. Why would she do that? What need would the Lycan Queen have to butter up the Centaur King?

Her heart began to race when she saw Colin and Roman lock gazes on one another. "That would be lovely. Thank you, Grace."

"Roman," Colin nodded toward him.

"Colin. Good to see you. I'm glad dinner is ready. I'm starving." He leaped from the couch and hurried to the dining table, claiming a seat and striking up a conversation with Zoltar immediately.

"Colin!" Wendy rushed into the room and threw her arms around her brother. Nala could feel the tension leave her mate, or at least she thought she could. Without a bond it was hard to tell if she were reading him right. "I've missed you. You look fantastic!"

He kissed her cheek. "I've missed you too. You look great yourself. Doing something different?"

She laughed and waved him off as she tucked her loose fitting purple dress under her legs and took a seat. "How are things in Belfast? Are the Gnomes situated? Thank you for taking them in. Both of you." She patted Nala's arm.

Colin looked to Nala and for once she knew exactly what he needed. "Oh, they're doing very well," she said. "Their homes are all built. Several of them are doing HVAC work, you know, running and repairing ventilation since it's easier with their size. Some are farm hands, picking fruit and nuts from trees, pulling weeds, that sort of thing. We have a few jewelers." She flashed her bracelet. "They do fantastic work. See."

"Wow, that's beautiful!" She ran her finger over the garnets on Nala's bracelet. "So perfect."

"Yes, it was a present from your brother." She smiled and nodded her head toward Colin.

"Well done little brother!" She smacked him on the

shoulder.

Nala continued with her distraction. "Honestly, they fit in just like anyone else. They're finding their way and they use very little resources. They've become quite the asset—a brilliant idea on your part."

Zoltar carried in two enormous serving trays, one in each hand and placed them on the table. "Dinner is served." He took the last remaining seat.

Nala kept a watchful eye on the table as everyone dished out their plates. She noticed Zoltar stiffen and Wendy's brow furrow. *Yep. They've bonded.* She looked at Grace who seemed to have heard her thoughts. Grace only gave a gentle smile and nod. This time her thoughts were directed at Grace. *He's not going to take this well, is he?*

"Truth is, none of us know, but we're all worried." Grace's voice came through loud and clear in her head which startled her. She stiffened in her chair.

"You okay?' Colin asked.

"Just a muscle spasm. I think I need to ease up on my workouts." She hated lying to him but wasn't about to disclose what had just happened.

"Wow, this chicken is delicious." Nala complimented Zoltar.

He lifted his glass of wine toward her. "Thank you."

Wendy put her fork down and grabbed Colin by the wrist. "Colin, I do have some news for you."

Oh shit! Here it comes.

Her face turned a few shades darker. "I love you. You know that?"

"Wendy please tell me what's going on before I scream."

She looked at her brother's pleading eyes. "Zoltar and I are mated." It came out as a blurt and then the table fell silent as they all stared at him.

Nala braced herself to restrain her husband if necessary. When his eyes flashed golden, she let go of her fork. "Colin."

He closed his eyes tight and looked back at his sister.

"Are you happy?"

A tear spilled down her cheek. "The happiest I've ever been."

He took a deep breath, held it for a moment before turning to Zoltar. "I'm sorry, my friend, old prejudices. You know?"

Zoltar held up his hands. "I completely understand. But I would never, ever hurt Wendy. We've bonded."

Colin's eyes widened. "I didn't know that was possible."

"That's not all," Wendy dabbed her eyes with her napkin. "We're expecting."

"What?" For the second time, the color drained from Colin's face.

"We're pregnant. Please, please say you're happy for me." She bit her bottom lip and held her breath as she stared at her brother.

Colin shot up from his chair and threw his arms around his sister. "Of course. Of course, I am. Don't cry. I just...please come see Doctor Maryann. Let her check you out. We have no experience with cross breeding. I only want to be certain you're healthy. That's all."

She nodded as he held onto her. "I was so worried you'd be upset with me."

Colin's husky laughter broke the tension around the table. "Since when has that *ever* been a concern of yours?"

A few soft chuckles went around the room.

"Thank God that's over!" Roman blurted. "Do you have any idea how worried I was that you'd read it on my face? We've known each other forever."

Nala breathed a sigh of relief as the tension left the room.

Colin extended his hand to Zoltar. "Welcome to the family, Brother."

The tears in the Centaur King's eyes shocked Nala. A King...showing vulnerability?

"Thank you. Now, after dinner, we have one more magical surprise. So eat up." Zoltar looked at Colin with hope in his eyes. "Don't worry, there's nothing to worry about with the last surprise."

Not having had much in the way of lunch, Nala was famished and had completely cleaned her plate before anyone else. She sipped her wine and followed the conversation, curious as to what the big after-dinner-surprise would be. Unsure of what other bombs Wendy could drop on her brother tonight, she settled on enjoying the company of others.

Grace was the reason she defeated Jagger and she'd never forget that. She was also the catalyst for her new status as Alpha over the Belfast pack. They'd joined forces in abolishing the High Council and Grace's most endearing quality, as far as Nala was concerned, was her desire to empower the women of the supernatural world. She fought for Nala's right to remain Alpha and orchestrated the merging of the packs. She really did owe her queen her life.

A year ago she was locked in a cage, a sex-slave to an abusive Alpha. Had anyone told her then that a year later, she would be Alpha, sitting at a table among royalty with her new husband and sister-in-law she would have rolled her eyes. But this was her new life and she couldn't have asked for more.

As soon as everyone had finished eating, they took their drinks onto the back patio area. Beyond the patio a small fire was lit in a fire ring. Colin had grabbed her free arm and looped it in his. "A lot to take in," he whispered. "Thank you for running interference."

"Ready for the big surprise?" she asked him in a low voice.

He shrugged. "Who knows? It can't be any bigger than their announcement."

She looked at him, noticing his eyes crinkling at the sides as he smiled. Seeing her mate happy lifted her heart.

As they made their way toward the fire, she noticed Wendy breaking off from the rest of them.

"Okay, ready?" Wendy had her hands on her hips.

"Enough already! Just tell me!" Colin gave a teasing growl.

The air around her shimmered for a brief moment before her head lifted higher in the air. When the air cleared, she was, from the waist down, a horse. Horse hair covered her from just above the breast down. Wendy was now a Centaur.

"Fuck me!" Colin gasped and fell back on the wooden bench.

"Don't worry, brother." Roman slugged him in the shoulder. "She can still shift to wolf."

Roman, Grace, Zoltar and Wendy had smiles on their face, but only for a brief second when they all stiffened and frowned.

"Party is over. Wendy, go inside." Zoltar barked. "Colin, come with us."

Colin looked just as shocked and confused as Nala felt.

"What's going on?" Nala asked.

Wendy shifted on the run, grabbing Nala by the arm, pulling her toward the patio doors. "We've been holding a Separatists prisoner in the basement. Barb went to take him his dinner and he was gone. He could be anywhere."

"Come on," Roman said to Colin. "Let's go find the bastard."

Nala could see the stress on Colin's face. He didn't want to leave his sister and mate alone.

She rushed over to him. "Don't worry. I'll protect her. Go."

Quite suddenly, his hands were on both sides of her face. He pulled her in and planted a kiss on her lips. If she weren't panicked and on guard, she may have melted, but this was not the time.

He shifted to wolf and followed the others while Nala locked the door behind her.

"Do you think he'd really come after you?" she asked Wendy who was holding a trash bin and looking very green.

"Zoltar and I haven't kept our courtship secret. I'm the

one who captured him, so it's likely he's out for blood." She heaved into the can. "I'm sorry. I'm so sorry. The nausea comes and goes."

She didn't have the heart to tell her that after all she'd seen in her life, a little vomiting wasn't going to turn her stomach. "It's fine. Why don't you sit on the couch and put your feet up. Try not to worry. You have three royals and a former Alpha out there. They'll find him."

Wendy plopped on the couch and tilted her head back. "I hate to ask favors here, but there are cans of Ginger Ale in the fridge. Would you please grab one for me? I might lose it if I move."

She hurried into the kitchen, grabbed the ale from the fridge and rushed back to Wendy's side, handing her the can. Dread filled her every cell. She hoped they'd all come back unscathed. She couldn't stand the thought of any of them getting hurt.

The lower part of the front door opened, causing her to jump. A female Gnome rushed in and ran straight to Wendy.

"You okay?"

"Yes, Mary. Thank you."

The little Gnome ran to the bathroom and came back with a damp cloth, placing it gently on Wendy's forehead.

"Nala, this is Mary, my closest friend. Mary, this is Nala, Alpha of my former pack and my sister-in-law." She closed her eyes and looked like she concentrated on her breathing.

Relieved to have someone there to care for Wendy's needs, Nala shook the little woman's hand. "Very nice to meet you. I just wish it was under better circumstances."

Boom! Boom! Boom!

Three loud noises came quickly. The room shook.

"No! Not again!" Wendy bellowed before vomiting once again.

"What was that?" Nala held on to the wall, her heart racing, and her ears pounding.

"We're under attack—again!" Wendy cried and heaved

into her pail once more.

"Separatists?" Anger bubbled up and heat circled Nala's neck. Why bomb a school full of children?

Mary hopped up on the arm of the couch next to Wendy and pulled her hair back, securing it with a pencil she had snatched off of the table. "Yes. The last time it was really just smoke and a tiny bit of fire damage. But I don't know if the walls will hold again."

Crack! The patio door cracked as something hit it. The second strike had it shattering into a thousand flying glass shards. A male wolf stood seething at the new opening.

"Get her to the bathroom. Lock the door." Nala ordered before shifting to wolf.

The second strike had it shattering into a thousand flying glass shards. A male wolf stood seething at the new opening.

She took a few slow steps so she was blocking the path to Wendy.

The wolf leaped toward her. When it collided with her, she bit a chunk out of its shoulder and whipped her neck, throwing the beast against the wall. Not waiting for him to recover, she jumped toward him again, this time, sinking her teeth into his throat, ripping it out of his body. Blood sprayed into her mouth, leaving a salty metallic taste. She dropped the disembodied throat on the floor and stared at the beast bleeding out in front of her.

Hearing glass scraping between the floor and paws she spun around to find yet another wolf. She sprang to action, charging at him. When she collided, he snapped at her face. She pulled her muzzle out of the way then snapped back as they rolled on the floor. She scrambled back to her paws. The wolf was bigger and stronger, but she'd had training now. No matter what, she couldn't allow him to pass. Wendy's life, and that of Colin's unborn niece or nephew were depending on it. Her mate needed her to be stronger than she'd ever been.

She dove, grabbing at his front leg with her teeth and yanking it with her, forcing him to fall onto his side. She took a chunk of fur out of him and bit again. A limping wolf was a less worthy opponent. The wolf shifted to human as she was biting his arm. Searing pain cut through her shoulder, burning as something sliced through her flesh. He'd stabbed her with a blade.

But she could fight as human too. She shifted, which significantly healed her wound almost immediately. Dropping her weight to her right foot, she spun, landing a hard kick to the breadbasket. When he doubled over she drove her knee into his face. He staggered, long black tendrils swaying in front of his face before he swung, landing a punch to her right ribs.

Blinding pain accompanied the cracking sound of her ribs. She couldn't let him get to Wendy. She had to push. Taking two fast but painful steps toward him, she threw her legs up, locking them around his neck and flipping him onto the ground as she pulled with every pound she had behind her. When they met the floor she rolled toward her back, nailing him hard in the nose with her elbow. He was out cold, but her ribs were broken.

When she noticed the third Lycan bolt into the room, she nearly panicked seeing the tiny Gnome standing in the hall between him and the door to the bathroom. The little thing was vibrating so hard she looked blurry. Nala had no idea if the little ones could defend themselves.

Bent in half from the pain in her ribs, she moved quickly as she could toward the wolf.

Mary bounced off the floor onto the wolf's head and began clawing fast and furious at the eyes. The wolf howled and screamed, shaking its head to get Mary off, but the little Gnome held on, growling furiously. She pulled something from her hair and stabbed the wolf repeatedly in the face. Its paws scrambled below it.

Despite the pain in her ribs, Nala reared back, landing the hardest kick she could muster into the ribs of the beast. It yelped and fell to the floor, shifting to human form.

Mary did not stop her assault however. She continued

stabbing as the man as she continued to scream. Nala's suit was completely ruined as she was already covered in blood. She grabbed a vase, smashed it and used the shard to slice the man's throat, spraying blood all over the walls and floor.

"Stay in there. Stay in the bathroom," she gasped as she tried to call out to Wendy. Every breath hurt, sending stabs of pain through her side accompanied by what felt like fire that licked through her chest. Her shoulder pulsed with pain. She had one good arm and two good legs to fight with...if she could just breathe.

After shifting back to wolf to try and heal, she nudged the little Gnome with her muzzle. Mary's eyes burned a demonic red. Nala wasn't frightened of much but that little creature looked terrifying. It caused her to take a step back. Shifting helped ease the pain in her ribs, but they still hurt.

"I'm okay," Mary gasped. She shook her head while blinking until her eyes cleared.

You're a tough little shit, I'll give you that much.

"Nala! Nala are you guys okay?" Grace's voice was screaming in her head. *"Wendy isn't answering."*

We need help, Grace. We've killed three so far. But I'm hurt.

Mary walked over to Nala and probed her ribs with her tiny fingers. "Poor thing, your ribs are even broken as wolf. You should be healing. This makes no sense."

All Nala could do was bob her muzzle. She fought back the pain as she stood guard over the bathroom. Why wasn't Wendy answering? She nudged the little Gnome with her muzzle again and motioned with her paw toward the bathroom.

"She passed out," Mary answered. "Hyperventilated, I think."

A Centaur, two enormous Lycans and her mate rushed through the broken door. The relief of having backup nearly made Nala howl. They rushed toward her. Colin sniffed her from her head to her rump, whining. Zoltar, however, rushed to the bathroom and gently opened the door. Wendy was passed out on the floor, though she'd managed to shift to Lycan. Nala wondered if it made her feel safer than being in the vulnerable human form.

Zoltar knelt down beside her, stroking her fur. "It's okay. I'm here. Wake up, Wendy."

Nala walked forward a few steps to give them a bit of privacy. She saw something move by the open hole that used to be the patio door. She let out a low growl, warning the others. A Werepanther stood in the opening, panting. She shifted immediately to a sobbing blonde who ran over to Grace, who had shifted in a split second.

"Oh my God!" The woman threw her arms around Grace. "Is she...is Wendy okay?"

Grace led the hysterical woman back outside.

Nala nudged Colin, wishing they had the mental connection to communicate telepathically. If they were bonded, it would be there. She limped forward, blinding pain in her side nearly too much to stand. She eased down on her haunches and sat.

Colin shifted back into his human form. "Nala? How badly are you hurt?" He looked around at the wreckage that had been his sister's home. Three dead wolves littered the living room.

Mary placed her hand on his forearm. "She's not healing like your kind do. As a wolf she was stabbed, then as a human, she had her ribs broken. I'd say she's in pain but probably feels best like this. Let me go find one of the Fae. They can help her heal." She turned and looked toward a groggy Wendy who was picking herself up off of the bathroom floor. "And check on her."

He nodded. "Thank you."

Nala watched as Mary rushed out of the little built in door. She let her front paws slide against the tile until she was on her stomach and then rolled to her side. The coolness from the tile helped ease the pain.

"Three wolves," he whispered in her ear, "very impressive, dear." She felt his hand gently stroking her fur, trying to offer comfort. "We'll get you better and get you home."

She wanted to know what happened. Did the prisoner get away? Who attacked them? What were they shooting at the school that rocked such an enormous building and did it attract the attention of the humans? All she had were questions and she couldn't even shift back to ask them.

"He didn't get away this time," Zoltar knelt down next to her.

You can hear me?

"Not very well. I'm only part Lycan, but it does come with the territory of being a royal." He looked at Colin. "She wants to be filled in. She has a lot of questions and she's afraid if she shifts back to human, it will hurt more than she can take." Turning back to Nala, he rested his palm on her head. "You're losing a lot of blood out of that shoulder. You may start to pass out. If you do, try not to panic. Help is on the way."

"Thank you. How's Wendy?" His voice trembled as he stared down at her shoulder.

Zoltar shook his head. "She was scared and sick. She bumped her head as she was passing out but I think she's fine." He went back to the bathroom and helped Wendy to the bedroom.

Colin continued stroking her fur as he spoke. "There is a group of shifters that are very unhappy about the integration, as you know, they attacked the school once before. They're calling themselves Separatists. The prisoner in the basement was captured during the last attack. Grace caught up to him and, well, put an end to him. A few of them got away, but we managed to kill the rest. They were shooting grenades at the building. Zoltar said they'll have to do some structural repairs. The students are obviously shaken, but a lot of them helped defend the school."

She let out a whine ad rested her head on the floor.

"Why aren't you shifting, Nala? Are you hurt that bad?"

Another whine whistled through her nostrils as closed her eyes, feeling the overwhelming desire to rest now that the threat had been eliminated…for now. Darkness crept in and she drifted off.

THREE

"She's bleeding internally," the large man said as his hands hovered over Nala's body.

Colin gulped.

"I can see she was stabbed somewhere in the back. I believe either the broken ribs or the stab wound has punctured a lung. You need to understand I can heal her somewhat, but she'll need medical attention when you get her home. Get her to your doctor and get some blood in her right away." He patted Colin on the back. "Your mate has a very clean and strong aura. She has a warrior's heart with a mother's tenderness, but she's been hurt. Not just physically now, but she's been hurt in the past. She's very guarded. That's going to make my healing of her a bit more difficult."

Colin stared at Nala as the man spoke. He didn't even see the hand on his chest.

"Please, just a foot. I need some space."

He scooted back, but remained on the floor, his eyes locked on his mate. The large man started swirling his fingers over her in tiny circles. Then he ran his hands along her body. Admittedly, Colin hadn't taken much time to get to know anything about the Fae. He didn't know what drawing circles on his mate's fur would do, but didn't care, so long as she healed.

Nala, while still unconscious, shifted back to her human form. Her suit jacket was gone. The light pink blouse she was wearing was soaked in blood along her shoulder where she'd been stabbed. Blood also spattered on her front, though it didn't look like it came from her. Her beautiful black hair was a knotted mess on the floor instead of in the flawless French twist she'd donned. She had bruises on her arms and her face. Mary was right; Nala had barely healed at all. Colin could only guess it was from whatever Jagger had used on them for so long to keep the women from shifting. It must have weakened their system.

It was only when he felt light headed that he realized he was holding his breath. He took a deep breath in and let it out. The large man kneeling over her body had to be nearly seven feet tall, though his strong hands made delicate movements. Then his fingertips illuminated and what looked like a blanket of energy came out of him and draped over her.

The man sat back on his heels and turned to Colin. "Take her home. Have your doctor take care of her and she should be okay in a day or so."

Grace and her friend came back into the apartment. The Fae man stood from his position next to Nala and glared at Grace. "I've warned you twice."

She only nodded in return and gazed at the floor.

The blonde next to her shook and backed through the opening in the wall. "I'll go back to my room."

As soon as she was out of sight, the large man who'd just been so tender with Nala took three very large, very deliberate steps toward Grace. Colin wasn't sure whether or not he should be on the defense of his Queen, or stay out of the situation.

The Faerie stuck his finger out at Grace. "Her aura is filthy. She is hiding something. I've told you twice before.

Get to the bottom of it, or get her out of here."

To Colin's astonishment, Grace hung her head instead of fighting back. "I know what she's hiding and it has nothing to do with this, I can assure you."

He took a step back, straightened his shoulders, then spun on his heel and stormed out of Wendy's destroyed apartment.

Colin scooped Nala up off of the floor. He looked at Grace and used his head to motion toward the door. "Can you get it? I'm going to get her back. And please, have my sister call me tomorrow."

"Of course," she said as she hurried to the door. "I'm sorry you two got caught up in this."

He shook his head. "It sounds like we're all caught up in this. Shit!"

"What?"

"I don't know where I'm going. I need to get to the car." He looked into the hall where students were running around frantic.

"I'll take you." Zoltar appeared in the doorway. As soon as he was in the hall, he shifted to his Centaur form. "Put her on my back then climb on behind her."

Normally, he'd never accept a lift from a Centaur. But his mate was injured and this was no time for pride. He lifted her, gently as he could manage, and placed her on Zoltar's back. He climbed on behind her, feeling awkward about riding the man. He put a protective arm around his mate, leaning her head against his chest.

"Grab my mane to steady yourself. Don't worry. It's not uncomfortable for me." As soon as Colin had a fist full of mane, Zoltar started trotting toward the end of the hall.

"Please take care of Wendy. I'm very worried. If I knew she wouldn't pitch a fit, I'd be taking her back with me tonight." He looked down at Nala's bruised face. "But I have to get my mate back for sure."

Zoltar looked over his shoulder at him. "I promise, my herd and I will protect her with my life. I never would have left her if I didn't think she was in good hands. I'm just sorry your mate is so badly injured. However, I must say I'm quite impressed. She took down three large males by herself."

Another Centaur was guarding the door. When Zoltar approached, the Centaur helped lift Nala off of him so Colin could get down without dropping her.

"Her pulse is strong," the Centaur said as he handed her back to Colin.

"Thank you." He didn't waste any more time with niceties. He rushed to the car, secured her in the passenger seat, leaning it back so her head wouldn't flop around before belting her in. Once in the driver's seat, he roared the engine and tore off down the long lane. So many emotions flooded through him he felt numb. His years as an Alpha taught him to control his emotions and do what needed to be done. But with his second mate mortally wounded, his heart was breaking. His hands shook and fast as his heart was beating. What would he do if he lost her too?

How was he supposed to be a strong Lycan and protect his wife, while submitting to her at the same time since *she* was the Alpha? How could he not jump in and protect her if someone challenged her for her seat as Alpha? A woman as a Pack Master was unheard of. She'd been the first in hundreds of years and many Lycans weren't happy about it. No one from their own pack seemed to question it, but they'd already received word...rumors of challengers. The Chicago pack had already outgrown their territory, split up and bought out Scottsboro. Would they try to claim Belfast too?

The thought made him nauseas.

He focused on the road ahead, trying not to drive too far over the speed limit. It would be difficult to explain Nala's condition to a human. She looked like a battered wife or kidnap victim and trying to convince a human of anything else would be a major challenge.

She stirred, moaning.

"It's okay, Nala. I'm taking you home. You're going to

be okay." He grabbed her hand and squeezed. "I'm right here."

She wrapped her right arm around her stomach and moaned once more before falling unconscious again. He felt her hand vibrating...shivering. Concerned that the blood loss was making her cold, he turned the heat on in the car, despite the seventy-five degree temperature reading.

The drive back home to the pack's land was nerve wracking and while it only took twenty-minutes, it felt like a lifetime. He carried her straight to Doctor Maryann who went to work immediately securing a blood bag and a saline IV.

"Her pulse is strong, but her blood pressure is down. I'd say she bled internally. Lung sounds are good, Colin. There's no reason to believe she won't be fine." She patted his shoulder. "Nala had me do bloodwork on her when she arrived. I compared that sample to a sample I just took. The foreign substance that keeps her from healing is cleaning out of her system. This won't always be the case. Okay? She will get better and she will heal like a normal Lycan."

He couldn't answer through the lump in his throat. He gave her a nod and a forced smile, hoping that would convey his gratitude.

"The human body shuts down during mass injury. That's why she's asleep. Sleep helps the body heal. Her wolf seems to be okay, but her human body took the most punishment. She'll more than likely wake hungry as hell in the morning. So be prepared to get her dressed and up to the house for some breakfast. Understood?" She headed out of the room, pausing at the door. She smoothed her hands on her white coat. "Colin, do try to get some rest yourself."

He gave her another nod. As soon as she closed the door behind her, he kicked off his shoes and pulled off his shirt. Careful not to tug on any lines or wires, he climbed into bed with her and slid under the blankets. He tried to relax and doze off but every time she moved, he couldn't help but do a quick assessment.

"She's strong. Our mate is just resting." His wolf tried to reassure him.

She moved again, this time rolling into him; putting her head on his shoulder and wrapping her arm around him. She'd been cold on the ride home and now seemed to need his warmth. After a soft kiss to the top of her head, he closed his eyes.

FOUR

Nala opened her eyes and realized her cheek rested on a bare chest. Sitting up, she saw Colin's face ease into a smile.

"Feeling better?"

After a quick assessment, she nodded. "Other than feeling like I could eat an entire steer by myself, I'm fine."

Colin pressed the call button on the bed. He stood and pulled his shirt on.

Doctor MaryAnn came in and began to pull the IV out. "How's our Alpha?"

The fussing over her made her uncomfortable. "If you'll get this stuff off of me, I just want to go grab some breakfast."

Once free from the IV and heart monitor, she stood from the bed.

"You'll be happy to know that this morning while you slept I took another sample of blood and compared it to the initial sample I took, as well as the sample from last night. I'd say within a week, the foreign substance should be completely out of your system." She wound the wires and hung them around the monitor.

"That's good news." Nala looked at her feet. No shoes. *Damn! I liked those flats.*

The doctor tucked her hands in her pocks. "As long as you're not in any pain, I have no restrictions. You seem to have healed completely."

Colin put his arm around Nala and gave a gentle squeeze. "That's fantastic. Now let's get up to the house and get you fed."

Once outside, she ignored her stomach. With a gentle tug on her mate's arm, she pulled him to a halt. "Thank you for taking care of me."

Wrapping his arms around her, he pressed his lips to the top of her head. "Thank you for protecting my sister."

His warmth enveloped her. Unwilling to let him release her just yet, she pulled her arms tighter around his waist. "She's my sister now too."

When he pulled back, the void of his warmth tugged at her insides. "I learned something very important last night and you need to know." He looked up to the sky and blinked before looking her in the eye again. When he did, moisture glistened, tears he tried not to let fall. "Bonded or not, I would be devastated if anything happened to you. Seeing you injured like that—I couldn't stand it. So it doesn't matter if you bond with me or not, I will suffer if I lose you."

Sucking her bottom lip in, she fought the stinging of tears in her eyes. "Breakfast," she croaked. She cleared her throat. "Let's get some breakfast and some clean clothes." After a deep, cleansing breath, she turned toward the house.

They continued to hold hands until they reached the house. Wide eyes greeted them, as the pack members saw their Alpha, covered in dried blood.

"What the hell?" Tracy ran toward her, looking her over. "Since when does dinner with the in-laws have this kind of outcome?" Glaring at Colin, she clenched her jaw.

Placing her hand on Tracy's shoulder, she drew her attention away from him. "There was an attack on the school. Most of the blood isn't mine." She turned to Colin. "Maybe we should take breakfast in our room."

He nodded. "I'll get it together and meet you up there so you can get cleaned up."

She turned to Tracy. "Have Jake call a pack meeting for five this afternoon." After a deep breath, she continued. "I will be fine. I am fine. Don't worry." She left the kitchen and trudged up the stairs to her room. After peeling her shirt off, she tossed it in the trash and grabbed a T-shirt. As gross as she felt, hunger overcame her desire to bathe.

Colin appeared with a tray of food and put it on the small table in the room.

They both ate quietly. Events from the night before flashed in her mind. The three wolves had been determined to get to Wendy. Now that she had offered sanctuary to the Gnomes, the Separatists might consider attacking them as well. It added an additional layer of concern for her. She now had to consider the safety of her extended pack, the Gnomes, and her position as Alpha. It wasn't a question of *if* she'd be challenged, it was only *when* and *by whom*.

When she was finished, she stood from the table. "Thank you for bringing all of this up here."

Her mind still wrought with concern, she turned and headed into the bathroom. She hadn't noticed Colin on her heel. She gave a jump when she saw him standing behind her.

"Intimacy before sex." His voice was low, considerate. Slowly, he reached toward the hem of her shirt and pulled it up over her head.

She looked up at him, his eyes focused on hers. Her hands shook as she lifted them, unbuttoning the first button on his shirt. *Intimacy before sex. What does that mean, exactly?* When she reached the last button, she pulled his shirt open. His form was something to be admired, toned and tanned, his chest strong; his stomach, hard and defined.

He helped her step out of her dress slacks and then tossed the ruined pants into the trash before turning back toward her. "You are a fierce warrior, able to handle yourself. But you are safe with me—always safe…with…me."

A dull ache started in her chest and radiated through her body. Suddenly her weight was too much to bear. She leaned in to him, her forearms on his chest, and her forehead at his collarbone. Thick armor shredded as relief washed over her in the form of large sobs. Safe. She hadn't felt entirely safe for years.

His arms wrapped around her, holding her tight. He never interrupted, never wavered—only stood firm and let her experience the relief she needed.

When she finished, he gently turned her back to him and unclasped her bra, then slid her panties to the floor. She heard his buckle hit the floor, and assumed they were now both completely naked. She stepped into the shower and closed her eyes as warm water poured over her head, rinsing the blood and dirt away. When she leaned out of the water, strong hands began massaging shampoo on her head. She closed her eyes and allowed herself to enjoy the moment.

Intimacy before sex.

A gentle push placed her head back under the water, rinsing away the suds. When she opened her eyes and turned to her mate, he had a gentle smile on his face as he filled his palm with conditioner. With his other hand, he twirled his finger, directing her to turn back around.

Their first time naked together and there were no nerves. She didn't feel bashful, not this way. He combed his fingers through her wet locks, ensuring the conditioner made it to the ends before rinsing off his hands.

He wasn't pawing at her or showing any sign of being disrespectful and it had set her at ease. Reaching up, she grabbed his loofa off the hook and squirted a little body wash on it. Keeping her gaze on his chest, she began spreading the suds over it, up his shoulders and down his torso, spotting his erection when she finally allowed herself to look. Though his body was aroused, he took his time, he was showing her intimacy. His words were making sense.

She walked around him, continuing to soap him up, using the loofa in one hand and spreading the suds around with her free hand. Admiring his strong backside, she continued to explore him, kneeling to soap his strong, lean legs.

When she stood again, he turned to face her. His thumb and index finger eased around her chin, he brushed his lips against hers with a light kiss. With soapy hands, he massaged her neck and shoulders, gliding his hands down her arms. She closed her eyes, reveling in the attention. When he pulled her against him, her heart gave a start. Their naked bodies were now pressed against one another, wet, naked…completely vulnerable.

He gave her that. He'd allowed her to sob into his chest, to show vulnerability without fear of losing her place…her respect.

Returning his embrace, she kissed his shoulder and rested her head on his chest as the hot water poured against her back. The squeak of the faucet echoed in the shower stall as he turned the water off. Releasing her, he stepped out of the shower and held his hand out for her. As if she needed steadying. She accepted his hand anyway. A chivalrous gesture shouldn't go ignored. Once they were both out of the shower, he slid the towel off the rack and began squeezing the water from her hair before toweling her off.

The odd feeling of someone else towel drying her made her feel awkward for the first time. She went to pull the towel up herself.

"Uh-uh. I'm taking care of you and you're going to let me." When he looked at her, she saw his golden eyes illuminate. He was emotional. When she was dry, he wrapped the towel around her before drying himself. With a quick movement, he grabbed her brush from the counter and led her to the bedroom.

Her heart rate increased and her legs began to feel shaky.

When she sat on the bed, he claimed the area behind her and began brushing through her hair. She closed her eyes. Each gentle stroke with the brush lulled her, like the sway of a crib to a baby. He took his time, gliding the brush through her dark hair. Then she felt him braiding it. *He's braiding my hair?*

"You know how to braid?" She snickered as she spoke.

He chuckled. "My mother had the most beautiful hair. I used to watch Wendy practice on her. I sort of picked it up. It's not really all that difficult."

She could hear the snap of the rubber band as he secured it to the end. He finished by kissing the top of her shoulder. Her stomach clenched.

He pulled her back against his chest and whispered in her ear. "If you want to stop, you must tell me."

She turned her head to the side and craned her neck so she could look at him. She bit her lip and shook her head. "No, I don't want to stop."

Leaning forward, he planted his sweet lips on hers. Her heart began beating so loud and so hard she heard it in her ears. She was ready. She wanted him…to be with him…to give herself to her husband. Their breaths increased as the kiss grew in passion.

A foreign sensation, something she hadn't felt in years exploded low in her belly. She was aroused. It had been so long, she barely recognized her very real need. Reaching her hand up, she wound her fingers into the back of his hair, pulling his kiss inward toward her. Her chest heaved as her heart raced.

His hands ran down her thighs and back up again then he slowed when he reached her stomach, taking his time, slowly making his way to her breasts, which felt full…heavy.

She gasped when he tweaked her nipple. Every cell, every nerve ending was on edge. She turned her body to face him and when she did so, he eased back on the bed. She climbed up until their lips met once more. She could feel his need hardening between them and for once she felt

46

anticipation to have it inside her. She wanted him...needed to be with him.

Fear took a back seat as pure desire took hold. Easing herself on him, her eyes instantly closed as she felt every inch of him slowly gliding in, her body stretching to accommodate him. She paused as her entrance met the base of his cock.

His warm hands caressed her arms, lazily rolled up her shoulders then tickled as his fingertips ran down her spine. With a shiver, she began to move easing up and down on him, relishing every exquisite inch of her mate. Control was hers until she was ready to relinquish it. He kept her pace, with gentle thrusts from below, continually massaging her from back to thigh as they made love.

Legs and arms quivered as a maelstrom overwhelmed her. Feelings for him ran deeper than she realized. She'd longed for this connection to him. Foolish was her desire to remain unbonded. It was his choice and not hers to take away. For far too long, her choices had been stolen and that wasn't something she wanted to do to her mate. A mate that was letting her take this giant leap at her own pace, showing nothing but tenderness and respect.

It was time to let go. She rolled off of him, pulling him with her. With Colin hovering over her, he showered her with kisses along her neck, nuzzling in before he resumed their lover's dance. She gasped with each thrust as he filled her to her core. Her breasts perked up to a point she felt they would burst as she met his thrusts, bucking her hips.

She licked his neck, tracing his throat with her tongue. A loan groan rumbled in his chest. A faint glow illuminated his neck above her. Her eyes were glowing, her wolf wanted out. Running her tongue along her teeth, she discovered her canines had elongated. This was it. It was time...time to let go and make the connection she so desperately wanted. He looked into her eyes, his glowing back at her.

Tears stung as her heart fluttered in her chest.

"Bond. Please, allow the bond!" her wolf pleaded. *"Our mate*

loves us."

He brushed his lips against hers and licked her lower lip. "Only if you're ready," he whispered.

Words evaded. She'd never be absolutely ready, but sometimes...sometimes you just have to take control. It was time to let go of her fear. She answered him by piercing his neck with her canines and felt the tiny pinch of his return bite.

In that moment, time came to a halt as a barrage of emotions overwhelmed her once more. Heartache, despair, loathing all crept in. *No! No, he hates me!* She began to push him off, but he held firm. Warmth, unlike any she'd yet to experience flooded her heart, then adoration, love, commitment, respect all flooded in like steel cables, holding her in place.

"I hated myself, but only for a brief second, my love." Colin's voice, his emotions poured out of him and consumed her. *"I am yours forever more. I am in love, truly, deeply, and completely. It was me, finally letting go that came in first. Please forgive my last stage of mourning."*

No more wondering what he was thinking or feeling, the connection was complete. To her surprise that wasn't all, she could sense...feel exactly what she felt like to him. How his cock felt against her inner walls. To him, she was warm, wet, and tight. Sensing her from his point of view overwhelmed her with a new kind of arousal.

He eased in and out of her. "Wow, I'll never get used to that."

Sensing lovemaking from both sides was a new experience...it had her on edge, pressure building. With both her hands on his hips, she pulled him in and bucked against him. She could feel his excitement, his pleasure coupled with her own.

The coupling caused them both to pick up the pace as he thrust into her, she cried out for more, as if he had more to give. He scooped his arms between her and the bed, holding her still as he planted his mouth on hers and pushed harder and harder. She moaned into his mouth, as her intensity built, she could feel his mounting until they couldn't last...until they couldn't stop. He pushed into her as they both cried out their orgasm.

He rolled off of her, but did not let her go. He pulled her into him, placing her head on his chest, her leg draped over his.

That was beautiful. She smiled as joy and relief took her. The sting of tears assaulted her eyes, the beauty of Colin's mind and soul invading her to her core.

"Yes, it was."

"Okay, you're voice in my head will take a little getting used to. But really, it feels so relaxing to know how you're feeling. To know that this isn't one sided." She stroked her fingers along his chest.

With a deep breath, he exhaled. "We can both relax." He kissed her forehead. "We're together forever, Nala. I felt you, your loneliness. You never, *ever*, have to feel that again. Do you understand? As long as I am breathing, you'll never be alone."

FIVE

Watching someone sleep while they're at their most relaxed and vulnerable, might seem creepy to an onlooker. But Nala studied Colin. As his deep heartache for his prior spouse eased, his heart made room for her. She didn't have to ask. She didn't have to guess, because now, she could feel it. He was elated to be her mate.

The biggest surprise for her was his fear of rejection. Though he tried to hide it, his mind spoke to hers; relieved she'd accepted him—wanted him for a mate.

Her cheeks pulled at her lips, pulling her usually taught lips into an easy smile. This might not be how she thought her marriage would go—her bond. She'd always thought it to be more rabid, during a heat, with dire need causing her to rip her mate's clothing to shreds as she took him continually until her need was at ease. This...was better. The bonding had been sweet. Their first time making love had been...romantic. Romance wasn't something in which she was well acquainted.

His elation had one strong, albeit negative side effect. More, now than ever, she had to work harder to be certain she would survive a challenge—many if necessary.

Burden.

She'd have to learn to turn of the heavy burden so her mate wouldn't know exactly how she felt most days. Sure, he'd understand. He'd been an Alpha with a family. But what would the rules be if she were with child? Would the challenge still be held if she were bursting with a pup inside her? How could she waddle around pregnant and fight to the death?

The gravity of her situation only weighed her down and burst the her post-coital bubble. Rolling away from her mate, she buried her face in her pillow, holding in a scream of frustration. Just like the rest of her life, she'd have to take it one day at a time, one foot in front of the other.

They had a meeting in just over an hour. A meeting regarding security, and security was of utmost importance. She left her husband to nap while she took another quick shower. Standing in her closet, she pulled the towel off her wet hair and hung it on the door before shimmying on panties. As she pulled on her jeans, she was startled by a gentle knock on the closet door.

"Are you okay? All I can feel from you is stress." Colin stood in the doorway, wearing only his boxers. His hair was a mess atop his head.

She shifted her weight to the balls of her feet as she stood topless in front of him. She looked at him for a second more than was comfortable before she pulled a bra around her arms. "I'm fine. We have this meeting about the Separatists and I don't want to walk down there a mess. The bite on my neck will tell the pack all they need to know." She hoped he'd accept her answer at face value.

After pulling a tank over her head, she saw her loving husband with his arms crossed over his chest. Okay, the bond. No more white lies. "A thought occurred to me and it upset me. Okay?" Just thinking about it felt like someone had punched her square in the stomach. "What happens if I'm challenged while pregnant? I mean, we haven't talked about…but still."

"That's simple. You don't fight. You name a proxy. It's what packs do to protect an elder, and a pregnant Lycan female is no different."

Of course it's so simple for you! How could she nominate someone else to die in her place?

"No. It's not. That would be my pup in there," he said pointing at her stomach. "An innocent. No one would stand for it, least of all me."

She reached in a drawer pulling out a fresh pair of socks and then pushed past him. "That's what I'm afraid of."

"Wait!" He grabbed her arm, spinning her around to face him. When she came to a stop, he slid his palms over her cheeks. "FOSE has just been established. We'll all have new laws to follow. There's no way on the planet Grace hasn't thought of this. If women are to rule, then pregnancy will be a factor in a challenge. Either the challenge will wait, or the Beta will fight. I know it seems more complicated but we have to cross that bridge when we come to it." He slid his arms around her.

She allowed herself to lean into him, allowed his warmth to envelop her.

"I told you. You'll never be alone again. You need to start believing me." He kissed the top of his head. "Now I'm going to take a shower. *You*…take five seconds and breathe." He left her standing there as he headed to the bathroom.

Breathe. Okay. She took a few cleansing breaths, then slid on her socks and shoes. Colin's words had eased her nerves somewhat, but an Alpha is supposed to care for her pack and it was a duty she took to heart. She wanted it…fought for it. *She* was a *leader*. Leaders don't lose their shit.

He stepped out of the bathroom with nothing on…not even a towel. When he crossed in front of her, he turned, shaking his butt in her face.

She burst into laughter and smacked his ass cheek. "Get dressed!"

"You're much prettier when you smile." He winked over his shoulder as he rubbed the red handprint on his butt.

Her heart skipped a beat every time her mate flirted with her. Secretly, she hoped it never went away. She focused on him as he stood in his closet, dressing. He was lighter. His smile seemed semi-permanent. She could feel a mixture of joy and frustration coming from him.

Still happy we mated? She pushed her thoughts to him.

"Absolutely. You?"

Indeed.

"I'm ready." Always dressed for a business meeting, he stood in dark blue pants, a white button down and dark shoes that matched his belt. He really did make her feel like a bum most days.

"Oh dear?" She said wagging her finger up and down at him. "I'd really love to see you in a pair of jeans occasionally."

Nearly all of his stunning white teeth showed when he smiled at her. "Yes ma'am!"

They made their way to the fire pit, where most pack meetings took place. She noticed numerous smiles from her original pack mates as they noticed her bonding mark. Nods of approval greeted them before the meeting began.

"It's with a heavy heart that I tell you all about a new enemy. An enemy of our own kind. It appears that not everyone is entirely thrilled that we're blending species. There have been two attacks on the school, one of which happened last night. The group call themselves Separatists, as they wish us all to remain separate. Let me just preface this by saying that I won't tolerate such racism. The Gnomes, who started out as our welcomed guests are now officially pack mates and have proven to be an invaluable resources. As Alpha of this pack I order you all to defend them as you would any Lycan brother or sister. I'm also quite pleased to tell you that they're far from feeble. I witnessed, first hand, the skillful warrior a Gnome can be when put to the test. The warrior I witnessed was both loyal and fierce." She turned to the group of Gnomes who sat together in the front of the crowd. "I'm quite proud to say that your friend, Mary, fought with precision and tenacity that would rival any Lycan I've ever seen. She defended my sister-in-law alongside me."

A collective gasp was heard around the group, followed by murmurs. She held up her hand to quiet the crowd. "Wendy Baker has been mated with the Centaur King. She's now the Queen and with child. Be certain to send your blessings. Now, on to security. These snakes like to sneak up in the cover of night. They shot bombs at the school as a distraction so they could get to Wendy." She turned her direction to Tom Johnson. "Tom, let's step up night patrols."

"Excuse me." One of the Gnomes, Joseph approached her. "We can set up motion sensors along the perimeter. I can set the sensitivity to ignore smaller animals. It'll still go off for, say a deer, but it's better than nothing. This way, we don't have to have so many of us out at night instead of in bed with our mates."

She looked to Tom who shrugged. "Seems like a sound plan. Maybe a few night-vision cameras too? Can you set those up to a monitor in my office...or something?"

Joseph nodded. "That'll be easy." He scratched the back of his head. "I think we can do it wirelessly. I'll have to see what I can get ahold of."

She smiled down at him. "Thank you. Please let Jake know if you need anything."

Her Beta stood at her side quietly, but nodded down at Joseph. "I'll get whatever you need. Just give me a list. Don't worry about cost."

She forced herself to stand a little straighter. "Now for the difficult part. If anyone of you here takes issue with our new ways of integration, speak now. I will not tolerate any less."

A couple stood from the back. She didn't recognize them, but she hadn't been around long enough to learn the names of her entire pack.

"Ma'am, it is a lot to take in. First, Colin steps down, then Roman succeeds him, but only for a short time then you're immediately our new Alpha. Now these little people are running around getting into everything and now Wendy is pregnant with a half-breed." He cleared his throat as he quickly glanced at Colin. "No offense."

She could feel the heat rising up her mate's chest, to his neck, then his face. He wanted to hit something.

"I'm sorry," she interrupted, "but I don't know your name."

The man lifted his chin. "Richard, this is my mate, Trina." He pointed to the woman next to him, who refused to look up from the ground.

"I see, Richard. Do you wish to leave?"

She watched as his eyes popped open wide.

"Excuse me?"

"If you're unhappy here, you may leave. I won't hold it against you." She narrowed her eyes.

"Leave our pack?"

She walked forward and knelt down in front of the group of Gnomes and whispered. "Would you all do me the kindness of standing next to Jake?"

With bobs of their tiny heads, then all scurried around until they surrounded the Beta. As soon as they took their place, she stood. "These are your pack mates. Will you defend them the same as you would my mate?"

He looked at his mate for guidance. She shook her head.

His voice was low, quiet and pitiful. "I'm afraid not."

You weak, sorry excuse of a Lycan. In a louder voice, she called out. "Anyone else feel that way?" When no one spoke she continued. "Say your goodbyes to Richard and Trina. They're going to go home and pack."

She chastised herself for not discovering this earlier so as not to have outsiders know of their security plans.

"I've known them my whole life, Nala. I wouldn't have guessed it. Don't beat yourself up." Colin's words came through loud and

clear, giving her some comfort and appreciation for their new telepathic connection.

"Did your Alpha stutter?" Jake growled as he stomped toward them. "Cowards! Pack up and go!"

After Richard and Trina ran toward their home, she approached Jake. "Have someone on them until they leave. I'll have Barry draft a check to cover the cost of the dwelling. I may want them gone, but I want to be fair as possible. Got it?"

"Done." A man of few words, he was already walking away the second her last word was spoken.

She called an end to the meeting and stayed behind with Colin while the pack members dispersed. "That was awful."

He stroked her back. "It was the right thing to do. Your job is to protect our pack. The Gnomes are part of it now. We survive as a collective, not as individuals." A soft chuckle rumbled in his throat. "It's for his own safety anyway. That remark about his sister put his dental health at risk. I was very close to ridding him of his teeth."

"Yeah, I felt your anger. It's going to take some getting used to handling my own emotions when yours are rolling into my mind. That was a low blow. I can't believe he said that." She cracked her neck. "It's almost dinner time. Let's head back to the house."

She turned to walk away when she felt his hand around her wrist.

"Nala?"

Turning to face him, she held her breath.

"You did the right thing."

Releasing her breath she nodded. "The right decision isn't always the most popular."

SIX

The mood was much lighter around the dinner table as smiles and polite conversation blanketed the room.

Jake joined as the meal was just about done. "Tom's with Richard and Trina now. There's a whole lot of screaming going on. I couldn't take it anymore." Shaking his head, he began piling food on his plate.

"Screaming?" Colin huffed. "By who?"

"Trina is mortified at leaving, chastising him for what he said about Wendy." He paused to look at Colin. "I wanted to break his jaw."

With a smile and a nod, Colin agreed. "Me too."

"Down boys!" Nala eyed them both. Two alpha males defending their sister's honor had more testosterone flying around the table than was acceptable.

Tracy interrupted the banter hurrying into the dining room. "Someone is approaching. Someone in a Jag."

Colin dropped his fork. "Dammit!"

When Nala shot her mate a look he rolled his eyes.

"Stephany Kincade, Roman's bitch-of-a-sister." Colin's mental words came with an onslaught of loathing. He really

detested the woman. The Alpha in her was on guard, the mate in her was relieved that her mate shared the same distaste for the woman. She'd only met her once before and the woman had been entirely dismissive and rude.

Standing from her seat, she tossed her napkin on the table. "Let's go greet her shall we? I'd rather keep that woman out of my house."

With a snicker, Colin stood, trying to hide his smile. "Yes, dear."

They met her in the parking area as she exited her black Jaguar. Her brown hair in a twist, dressed like she had an appointment in court. Her suit, a little too tight for her figure, pushed her boobs up toward her neck.

Nala crossed her arms over her chest. "Ms. Kincade, to what do we owe the pleasure?"

After she swung the car door closed she jerked both hands up by her shoulders and walked around the car.

Nala and Colin snickered as they watched her wobble. Her high heeled boots didn't maneuver well through the crushed stone.

"Ah, Mrs. Baker, Mr. Baker." Her blood red lips opened into a wide smile, displaying capped teeth that were too white to be real. "I got word that you were disposing of a few pack mates."

That was fast. Wonder how she heard? She pushed her thoughts toward Colin, while maintaining a face stiff as stone.

"Trina might have called her. They used to be friends."

"Yes, we've asked Richard and Trina to leave. Are you looking for new pack mates? My understanding was the Chicago pack had already outgrown themselves." She allowed a small smile to spread across her lips.

"Oh dear." She looked Nala from head to toe, "you really do dress for comfort." Turning to Colin, she plastered her fake smile on once more and put a hand on his shoulder. "Well, there's so much to do at Scottsboro. What a dump. We could use a few lower Lycans for labor."

"Lower Lycans?" Nala narrowed her eyes.

Stephany waved her off. "Don't take offense dear. Stature is stature."

Memories of cages and shackles flashed before her eyes. She blinked as she tried to regain her composure. "So Richard and Trina will be members of the Scottsboro pack then...under your protection?"

"Stay calm. She's trying to goad you." Her mate's warning suddenly having her regretting not taking a more diplomatic approach with Richard and Trina. Perhaps they could have been brought around. The thought of them going to live with the harpy standing in front of her made her feel ill.

"My protection? That's cute. They'll contribute to their pack and make themselves useful or they can find another pack." Looking around behind her she said, "Where are my little ragamuffins anyway?"

Looking at the twist at the back of Stephany's head, Nala fantasized ripping each hair from the root. "They're packing."

"Well am I just supposed to stand out here and wait like a vagrant?" She crossed her arms under her boobs. "Or are you going to invite me in?"

Not a second too soon, Richard and Trina rounded the corner in their pickup truck, which was sagging under the weight.

"Looks like you won't have to wait after all." Colin flagged them over.

The truck creaked as it rounded the corner and came to a stop. "Stephany!" Trina waved. Nala noticed the swollen and red skin under her eyes where she'd been crying. Guilt crept up until she felt as if she were choking on it.

After a deep breath, she walked over to the open window. She looked at Richard, who refused to look at her, then to Trina. "If your position changes, understand that our door is open. So long as you have such a distaste for the newest members of our pack, then it's the whole pack that is my priority." She cleared her throat. "A check for the value of your home will be mailed to you."

Trina nodded and sniffed. "Thank you."

"We'll be fine," Richard grumbled through his clenched jaw.

Looking over her shoulder at Stephany who was fighting not to twist an ankle as she made her way to the truck, she turned back to them. "I'm not so sure. Just remember what I said."

"I'm in the black Jag over there," she said pointing at her car. "Just follow me to Scottsboro." Looking at the truck she sighed. "Will this thing even *go* the speed limit?"

The arrogance and insults were grinding at Nala to a point she couldn't stand. If this particular bitch didn't vacate the premises soon, she'd have to show her exactly why she dressed for comfort.

Maxine, one of the Gnomes ran toward them with a box in her hand. Her red curls bounced as she ran, calling out. "Wait!"

Stephany spun around and looked down screaming. "A rat!" She kicked her leg at Maxine.

Nala threw her left leg forward colliding with Stephany's, whose foot narrowly missed hitting Maxine in the face. Grabbing her by her throat, Nala growled. "Do not ever assault one of my pack mates or I will rip out your throat. Do you understand?" Her chest heaved as furious anger boiled in her veins.

"Are you mad! What is that thing? Let go of me!" She pulled at Nala's hand, trying to release the tension on her neck.

Colin's warm hand rested between her shoulder blades. "I think you made your point."

"That *thing* is a Gnome *and* a pack mate. It looks nothing like a rat. Apologize to Maxine or I'll crush your windpipe." A loud growl bubbled in her chest.

"I'm so sorry," Maxine yelled. "I didn't mean to startle her. Please, Miss Nala, I'm okay."

Releasing her grip she stepped back. Stephany coughed

as she slid down the truck, rubbing her neck.

Maxine lifted her arms, stretching so that the little box was near the truck window. "This is to say we're sorry. We really must have failed getting to know you for you to dislike us so much. I wish we could have been friends."

Fighting the urge to pick up the little Gnome and squeeze her in a bear hug, she smiled and took a knee. "That's very generous of you."

Richard snagged the box and threw it at Trina, who gasped when she opened it to see a large ruby ring. "Oh my. It's beautiful." She smacked Richard with the back of her hand and proceeded to cry.

Turning to Colin, she set her jaw. "Get that filth," she tossed her head back toward Stephany, "off my lawn."

She stormed off toward the house, seething. *How could anyone be so fucking rude?* It touched her heart that the Gnomes, even after being dismissed by Richard and Trina, still wanted to give a peace offering…to show their good nature. Lower Lycans? She could only guess whatever classified someone as a lower Lycan, meant that they were not treated as well as the rest. What did 'lower' infer? Low quality? Lesser bloodline? It sickened her, the thought of two pack mates leaving to go to that.

Reaching the forest edge, she stopped, closing her eyes. The collective…that was her concern. She couldn't worry too much about two pack mates that refused to cohabitate with the others. When Grace proposed integration, Nala agreed with the best of intentions—to protect them as well as elevate their pack's diversity. She wanted to be a leader in the new paradigm. But her decision forced out two pack mates that may have otherwise lived the rest of their lives as part of the Belfast pack without incident.

Top that off with the assault on the Beta's wife of what was certain to be a rival pack, and she had a mess on her hands. Stephany had no pride. She'd run back to Scottsboro insisting someone come for her head…only hours after she finally bonded with her mate.

The Gnomes weren't guests any longer. Not only were they not a burden, they flourished into peaceful assets among their Lycan counterparts. They had huge hearts for tiny creatures, often foregoing sleep so new mothers could rest, working extra hours helping the farmers, so that they could be with their family. They made do with what they had, never complaining or asking for a thing. Their only request was to live above ground in actual homes and to be part of a community. Who could begrudge them of that? Who could think that these wonderful little people should freeze to death because a small fire would draw the attention of the humans?

She needed to talk to her King and Queen for guidance. She'd place the call after dinner. She'd gone this far on her own, but with integration, she needed direction. Any Alpha would have the same questions, the same challenges and the same concerns. The fact that she was a female Alpha shouldn't matter. Smart Alpha's often seek counsel from elders…this should be no different. So why did she feel like a failure?

Because Scottsboro wouldn't stay in the past. Because Mr. Kincade would be coming for her, of this, there was no question in her mind.

SEVEN

The next morning before breakfast, Nala spoke with Colin and he agreed to return to McGovern University and talk with Roman and Grace. He made mention of checking in on Wendy while they were there.

Dressing for comfort, she felt she'd rather not run the risk of ruining more dress clothes in case the school went under attack once more. Colin seemed to have understood. That, or he kept his wife's request in mind, because he dressed in jeans and a black, form fitting T-shirt.

"Now that's what I'm talking about. I knew you'd look good in a pair of jeans." She winked and nudged him, hoping to lighten the mood. She could feel anxiety rolling off her mate, though his thoughts were quiet. It drove her mad wondering what he was thinking again. Really? What good was having a mental connection if she still had to wonder what was on his mind?

"Actually, I'm just sort of…numb. All I keep seeing is my sister on the floor of the bathroom. I haven't had a coherent thought all morning." He blinked a few times then shook his head.

Running the tips of her fingers along his hairline above his ear, she smiled. "That was nausea. Pregnancy is a real bitch from what I understand. Don't worry. There's no way Zoltar will let anyone near her. She has an entire herd of Centaurs standing guard from what Grace said on the phone." She cleared her voice and took a step back. "I'm sure if they needed help, they'd ask."

With a light chuckle and a roll of the eyes, Colin shook his head. "You don't know my sister. Stubborn runs in the family."

They stopped in to let Jake know they were leaving before heading to the car. Nala had confidence in her Beta's ability. He never overstepped and showed loyalty to her almost immediately. Whether that was due to her position as Alpha or half-sister-in-law, she didn't know, nor did she think it mattered.

Once in the car, she began to relax. The drive there was more comfortable this time, with her mate opening up, talking about the past when he and Wendy were children.

"It was like having an older brother. She used to push me around a lot. Don't get me wrong, she never bullied me, not Wendy. She's too busy being a mother to *everyone*." His eyes crinkled at the side with this smile and it pulled at her heart, filling her with warmth.

"So what did she do?" She asked as she rubbed her fingers in his palms. Holding hands with him had been her first step toward intimacy and it was something that felt nice to her. She often held his hand when she needed to feel a connection. She imagined Wendy cutting big chunks of blond hair off his head, or moving his chair as he went to sit.

"Something she still does, though not many people catch it, when we're at the dinner table and she's walking around to serve, she'd flick my ear. You know, playfully mean, but it never really hurt. That kind of thing. You know, a gentle reminder that she is my *big* sister." He laughed while giving her hand a squeeze. "She used to put extra Brussel sprouts on my plate too, because she knows I hate them."

She wrinkled her nose. "Well, we have that much in common." Closing her eyes as she smiled, she leaned back in her seat, reveling in the sunshine coming through the window. It had been a few days since she'd went on her morning run and she missed that brief moment she took each morning…just closing her eyes and absorbing nature.

"Damn this is the longest driveway on the planet," he complained as she sped down the path.

Straightening in her seat, she took a deep breath. The vulnerability she showed with her mate would have to take a back seat during this important business meeting.

Zoltar and Wendy stood in the parking lot to greet them. Wendy looked good as new and radiant. The bump in her belly was starting to show as her shirt stretched to accommodate her tummy.

"You look fantastic!" Nala embraced Wendy for a brief moment before releasing her. The woman just oozed warmth and affection and it was something Nala really loved about being around her. "Motherhood suits you."

Zoltar shook her hand, then Colin's. "Welcome back."

"It's about time!" Wendy shrieked noticing the bonding mark on Nala's neck. "Good for you, little brother!" After wrapping her arms around his shoulders and squeezing, she kissed his cheek five times before releasing him.

"Now," Wendy wagged her finger at him, "before you even ask, the doctor said the pup is fine. We're both very healthy and I'm no worse for the wear."

The feeling of relief from Colin washed over Nala. She felt she could even breathe easier, which told her that her poor mate had been overwhelmed with anxiety he was trying to hide from her.

"That's really great news." He looked to Zoltar. "You're keeping up patrols?"

He gave one firm nod. "I have at least three of my men guarding her at all times. There is round the clock surveillance and nightly patrols. They won't hit the school again, not without one hellova fight on their hands."

Colin smacked him on the back. "That makes me feel a little better."

"We're going to meet in Grace and Roman's apartment. This way," Zoltar said as he held his arm out to guide them.

Wendy looped her arm through Nala's, who fought the urge to jump. Leaning toward her, Wendy whispered, "I'm very happy for the both of you."

Unsure how to respond, she smiled and looked over at Colin before turning back to Wendy. "Thank you. So tell me, how's the nausea? Any better?"

"Oh yes! The Pixies gave me some ginger root to chew. It's a little spicy but it really does the trick. The doctor says that it should be subsiding any time now." Lowering her voice to a whisper, she continued, "I'm having weird cravings though. Yesterday, I wanted pumpkin pie and pickled herring. It sounds absolutely revolting, but it's what I wanted."

"Yuk." Nala snickered. "That does sound repulsive."

"Here we are," Zoltar said as he stopped in front of a door. He knocked twice.

Roman opened up the door. "Hello. Grace is in the back, cleaning like a maniac."

Colin opened his arms and the two hugged briefly. "Good to see you. I miss you around Belfast."

"Not as Alpha dear. No offense. He's my friend."

None taken. Colin's use of their connection made her heart jump. Suddenly, she felt soft, like room temperature butter.

True to Roman's words, Grace was scrubbing the table like it hadn't been cleaned in a decade. "Hello, Grace." Nala stood a little straighter in front of her queen.

"Come, sit." Grace flagged them over and then took one more swipe with a towel.

She tensed during the small talk, eager to find the answers to her questions. When it was finally time, she filled them in on the events of the previous day. "The problem is,

I'm not worried about them. Apologies, Roman, but I really do not trust your sister."

He held up his hands, "No offense taken. Don't trust her at all. She's always been power hungry and offensive to anyone she deems less worthy."

"She referred to them as lower Lycans. I don't know what that means, but the connotation makes me very uncomfortable. My biggest fear is that I sent Richard and Trina to bowels of hell." She took a deep breath. "This isn't a challenge the Alphas before me have faced. Couple that with the fact none of us have heard from FOSE, I don't know how to proceed. We're not just a pack of Lycans anymore. But we are a pack and I need to know what the best thing is for my pack. So I'm seeking your guidance." She folded her hands in her lap and lifted her chin. Admitting her need for help was a difficult pill to swallow. Alphas are prideful. It is one of their qualities. But pride and humility had to dance in harmony for an Alpha to be successful, to have a healthy and protected pack.

"FOSE has had their hands full with the Separatists issue. Very little has been done to regulate integration. There are no clear cut rules for us yet." Roman looked to Grace. "I think she should put the whole pack first without concern for those who cannot adapt. What do you think?"

She closed her eyes for a moment. Nala noticed Roman did the same. She looked to Colin, pulling together her brows. *Nap time?*

Grace opened her eyes, the violet in them glowing. "The memories of our elders are vast. It takes concentration sometimes."

She cringed, having forgotten that her King and Queen could read her mind. She took a deep breath and held it in as she tried to hide her embarrassment.

They opened their eyes. "Proceed as you have. If any Lycans dare threaten the cohabitation with other species, they are to be excommunicated. It sends a solid message that we are moving forward as a cohesive society. There's a risk of creating animosity, or even more separatists. But we cannot allow threats to hold us back." Grace took a deep breath. "You've done the right thing. Hopefully Richard and Trina will come to see the error in their judgement."

Roman cleared his throat. "We will look into the Scottsboro pack. Like you, Nala, I do not trust my sister or her husband. The Chicago pack prescribes to the hostile takeover method of expanding their packs' territory. She'll not be content with her mate as Beta for long. Make no mistake, their pack is greedy and money hungry. Scottsboro is very humble in comparison to Chicago. They've been far from nature for entirely too long."

Grace patted Roman's hand. "It's okay. I'll say it." She turned her attention to Nala. "Should she challenge you again, show no mercy. Do not hold back for fear of my mate's feelings. No quarter."

"Are we maintaining an Alpha challenge as a no quarter competition?" Colin's voice cracked a bit toward the end.

Grace stood. "There's no reason it has to be," she paused and looked to Nala, "but it's unlikely someone will accept if you concede. There are many that are unhappy with a female as Alpha, Nala. You have to know this. You will be challenged and they will want to fight to the death to be certain all other females know their place."

Her stomach flopped. She already knew this to be true, it was no surprise. Hearing from the queen was a different matter entirely.

"And if she were with child?" Colin's voice was raspy, as if he choked on his words.

"The Beta may take her place," Roman interjected, "the same as when an elderly Alpha is challenged."

That didn't bode well. Nala's choices were to risk her life and the life of her would-be pup or her brother-in-law. How could she have put Colin in this position? Avoiding her mate's gaze, she looked to Wendy, the life growing inside of her. She wanted to same but that desire was selfish.

"Rest assured, we will be bringing this issue before

FOSE. They need to get the new laws and repercussions in order so we all know how to proceed. This far, most of this has fallen on Grace and while my queen is smart and resourceful, she hasn't *all* of the answers." Roman winked at Grace.

"That's what you think!" The playful tone in Grace's voice had calmed Nala to some extent, but she had more questions than answers. More dread. More fear. More concern for Colin.

The meeting took on a casual tone as Zoltar began pouring wine. Grace had prepared plates of fruit, cheese, crackers, and sausage ahead of time. Wendy sipped at iced tea, shooting smiles at Colin whenever he glanced her way.

Nala cleared her throat. "I was wondering if my new sister-in-law would be up for a walk?"

Wendy grinned as she placed her tea on the table. "Are you kidding me? I'm surrounded by unbelievable amounts of testosterone every day. I'd love some girl time."

"Not alone!" Zoltar's jaw flexed and he gripped the armrests of his chair.

"Oh for heaven's sake, Z, it's broad daylight and the whole herd is out today. Nala's a warrior. She's not going to let one hair on my head succumb to damage." She shook her head. "Honestly, it's like having a nursemaid on my heel twenty-four-seven." She walked over to him and kissed his forehead. "I love you."

Shaking his head, he looked up at her. "I don't have to like it."

Laughing, she patted his shoulder. "Nope. You don't. But I'm going."

When Nala stood, she faced Zoltar. "There are three royals here, and I'm bonded with the other Lycan in the room. You all have a connection with us. If anything should even smell something wrong, I'll call for help. Okay?"

Wendy grabbed her forearm. "Oh come on. He won't even let me pee in peace anymore. He'll have to be okay with it." She blew a kiss over her shoulder as they left the apartment.

"So," Nala started as they made their way out of the school, "I take it he's been a bit overprotective since the attack?"

"That's an understatement. I wasn't kidding about using the bathroom in private. He checks on me every ten seconds."

She imagined Colin acting the same, fussing over her every move until their pup was born…if they ever had any.

Once outside, they both looked around. Nala was scanning the area for any sign of threat.

"Come on," Wendy pulled at her arm, "there are beautiful trails in the forest."

Her arm felt warm where Wendy connected with her. The only other Lycan to exude such warmth for her was her mate. She wondered if it weren't something in their blood or if it was a familial connection now that Nala was a member of their family. Whatever it was, it seemed to turn her insides to mush and her shoulders relaxed from their usual tense position.

"Are you going to start talking or am I supposed to make small talk until you get the courage to ask what you want to ask?" Wendy snickered as she looped her arm through Nala's. "I know it wasn't a leisurely stroll you wanted, though I do appreciate it."

Had she been that transparent? "Well, uh," she cleared her throat as she searched for the right words. The trees covered the path like a lush green canopy. The forest was so full of life, so full of energy. It gave her the burst she needed to let her guard do. "It's not all subterfuge. I do want to know you more intimately now that I'm so connected to your brother, but I do have questions and…I don't know where to turn. My mother has been gone since I was young. My life before coming to Belfast, was all about survival. Now that I'm thinking about family, I'm a little lost." *That wasn't so hard.*

Wendy gripped her arm a little tighter and patted her

forearm with her free hand. "Anything worth having comes with risk. We risk ourselves when we fall in love. We risk loss. Becoming a mother means you might lose your child. Some children don't even survive birth. It's just a fact of life. None of us have any guarantees, sweetheart."

She chewed her lip as she contemplated Wendy's words. "How do you cope with it? How do you cope with your relationship and your pregnancy making you a target?"

Wendy snickered. "Lots of sex."

"Wendy!"

Continuing to laugh, she rolled her eyes. "Honestly. I am one hundred percent in love. After years of wishing for it, then accepting I'd probably always be alone, love finally happened. If I have to fight to the death to keep it—then so be it."

Her heart dropped into her stomach. "But...Colin has already lost a mate and a child. I don't want to put him through that loss again. It could destroy him." Her bottom lip quivered at the thought. "I can't do that to him. Not again."

Wendy stopped in her tracks and pulled hard on Nala's arm, spinning her around. She put her finger in Nala's face.

Nala felt her eyes widen, shocked at the authoritative stance of a woman who was usually so sweet and tender.

"Listen here, Nala Baker! You have one life to live. Just one! You're now bonded to my brother. He is in love with you and you clearly are in love with him or you wouldn't give two shits about his well-being. But that means you cannot rob him of his chance at fatherhood. You married. You mated. You bonded. It is done. Whatever fate has in store is out of your hands. You can't control everything. At some point, you have to let go. It was a freak accident that took his first wife and child. A freak accident! No one was out to kill her. There was no malice. It was just her time— as excruciating a thought as that may be."

Wendy's face was red and moisture glistened in her eye. "It was horrible. I'm not going to lie. But if you get pregnant, Jake can handle a challenge. He's good Lycan stock—quick on his feet—stronger than most. If you get pregnant, you allow him to step in. That's how this works." She put her palm on her forehead and stepped back. "I'm sorry, that was entirely too emotional. It must be the hormones. But I'm serious." She stepped in, forcefully wrapping her arms around Nala. "You must understand that this is *his* choice too. Don't take that from him."

Her shoulders relaxed as she wrapped her arms around Wendy, hugging her back. "Thank you."

"It must be exhausting worrying about everyone and everything all of the time. I have other royalty here, and those that I am so familiar with. But you're not alone. My brother's blood now runs through your veins. That means you are my sister. Nothing can take that away—not even death."

Death was the devil dancing in the corner.

EIGHT

Back home in Belfast, Nala stood in the bathroom, staring at herself in the mirror. Wendy had given her a lot to think about. Had she spent so much time trying to protect her mate from loss that she was robbing him of life?

"Yes," she heard Colin's soft voice behind her. "You're protecting me to death."

Staring at his reflection in the mirror, she noticed the smirk...Colin's typical half smile with lines forming around his eyes. It churned her heart into a puddle of primordial soup.

"What's wrong? Did you forget about our connection so quickly?" He stepped toward her.

She turned to face him, biting her lip. "Actually, I'm not really noticing it much. I thought it would be stronger than this."

"It is. You're coming through loud and clear. I've been sort of guarded so as not to overwhelm you. Keeping my mind distracted...you know, so you could focus." He wrapped his arms around her waist, gently easing her toward him. "I'm wondering if my mate wouldn't join me for a drink by the fire."

Expecting a kiss, she was delighted when he pulled her in a tight embrace…into a hug she so didn't know she so desperately needed. Her shoulders eased down as his warmth enveloped her.

"You're not alone anymore, Nala. There are no burdens that are only yours. Please, allow me to be here for you. Allow yourself a moment to relax. You have a whole pack here, *and* a mate. We are here for you. *I* am here for you."

Walls that had been firmly cemented in prior years started to crack as something stung her eyes. She felt her shoulders shudder and her chest heave as a light sob escaped her lips. "I'm sorry," she whispered in his ear. "I don't remember the last time I—" Her chest felt as if it had splayed open for the world to see.

"Do *not* apologize to me. If anyone understands…I do." His voice was low, near a whisper, yet it cracked at the end, a hint of emotion spilling over. "I am honored to be your mate. You can cry on my shoulder any time. In this space, you are not an Alpha. In this space, you are my wife."

I could stay here forever. His strong arms, warm and loving, wrapped around her made her feel safe and secure.

"And you will." He pulled away from her to look her in the eye. "About that drink?"

Nodding, she grabbed a tissue to clear her eyes. "I really do love you, Colin."

"And I love you, Nala. I hope by now you can feel it." He stroked her hair and smiled.

After clearing the lump out of her throat, she splashed cold water on her face and blotted it dry with a towel. "Drinks it is."

Once sitting together by the bonfire with wine in hand, he wrapped his arm around her waist. A few other Lycan couples sat around the fire conversing in their private twosomes. "So, my sister is going to birth a Centaur baby."

"Does that bother you?" She studied his face, illuminated by the fire.

"It's just weird. I mean…Wendy is true mother material and I want a family for her. I just can't wrap my head around my sister's status as a Centaur Queen. How in the heck could I?" After a big gulp of wine, he continued. "This is the same woman who flicks me in the ear."

She held in a giggle as long as she could before letting it go. "Colin! She's *a* Queen, not *your* Queen. It's okay that to you Wendy is just your sister, and Zoltar your brother-in-law. It isn't like you have to kiss a ring or anything."

His words were near a whisper as his expression fell blank. "She's having a baby." His emotions were a confused mixture of elation, envy, and sadness. He wanted a child and should have already had one had nature not taken it away from him. Her heart ached at her mate's turmoil.

"I've always wanted children," she whispered in his ear.

"But?"

"But I'm completely terrified." That was it. She'd finally come clean. "I will be challenged. I may die. If I happen to be with child, your brother would step in and he may die. It seems no matter what you are the one who suffers and I just can't live with that."

Pressing his lips against her temple, he inhaled her as he kissed the spot. "You don't know my brother very well. Don't assume that either you or he will lose. I guess I should have prepared you better, as my Alpha prepared me."

She turned to face him. "What on earth are you talking about?"

"The history. I'm sure they didn't teach you much of it in Scottsboro." He sat a little straighter. "The thing about a challenge is…usually the righteous is the victor."

Her shoulders slumped. "You've lost me."

"Throughout our history, the only challengers who've won have been those with a real need, a real passion to win and virtue on their side. There are been too many instances of smaller, weaker Lycans winning a battle they should have lost. It's almost as if the gods forbid anything less."

She shook her head. "Then explain Jagger. He was as

evil as Lycans come."

"Ah yes, but that wasn't a challenge. Your story was that he killed the previous Alpha in cold blood." He crossed his arms over his chest and crossed his feet at the ankles. "Why the Alpha didn't see it coming, I do not know, but that wasn't an outright challenge."

His words did little to soothe her concern. "Colin, I could just as easily fall victim to…"

"Is it possible that we have more faith in you than you have in yourself?" Tracy pushed her shoulder as she passed.

Nala bit her lip. "I worry. I worry all of the time about all of you, about me," she tossed her thumb at Colin, "about him. I wouldn't say it's faith as much as concern."

"Well you can stop worrying about me. I'm not a delicate flower." He looked at her, lips tight to hide his smile. "And the rest…well, we will cross that bridge when we come to it."

"There's no way in hell Jake would lose a challenge, or that any of us would allow a challenge while you're with child. So…can we revisit that issue soon?" He wiggled his brows as he pushed his thoughts at her.

Thomas and his wife Wanda joined them by the fire. They were carrying two sticks with marshmallows and immediately began roasting them by the fire.

The smell wafted toward Nala. "Oh that smells wonderful."

"We have more in the house if you'd like. I could go grab them." Tracey offered. When Nala nodded, she shifted and ran toward the house, returning with the bag and a few sticks. Colin made quick work sharpening the ends with his pocket knife.

Thomas and Wanda took turns feeding the gooey treat to each other. Wanda giggled with every bite that dripped down her chin. The scene was so sweet it warmed the Alpha's heart. The Gnomes generally didn't show much affection in front of the Lycans. This was the first occurrence Nala had witnessed.

"Love is a beautiful thing to witness, is it not?"

With a large smile, she gave her mate an affirmative nod. After a few marshmallows, they turned in for the night.

They'd barely crossed the threshold to their room when he grabbed her, startling her with a kiss. His hands pulled on her ass hard, crushing her into him. Prior to bonding, this may have started her, but the man felt a strong need for her, to please her, and nothing else.

His hands moved around to the front of her shirt and pulled hard, tearing it in half. Her back met the wall as he pushed her with no more force than someone closes the refrigerator. She was putty in his hands.

She raked her fingers down his shoulders, giving him a physical sign of approval. It was all he needed as his fingers pulled her bra material below her breasts, freeing them. He took her right nipple in his mouth as he undid her jeans. Her eyes rolled back as his tongue flicked her erect nipple.

He slid down, licking his way to the waist of her pants before jerking them to the floor. Nibbling his way down her hip, he used his shoulders to part her legs, diving between them to taste her. When his tongue parted her folds, her legs began to quiver.

The warm wet sensation pulsing on her clit made every nerve stand on edge. A far cry from the tender, sweet, first time, this was carnal in nature. Her body responded, her hips rocking, synchronized with the caress of his tongue.

She fisted his hair in her hands, holding on as the pressure built. His right hand slid over her ass, thumb gliding over her slit picking up moisture and gliding it to her behind. She tensed for a moment as her orgasm came to the precipice. When his thumb, slick with her juices, glided over her ass again, she was stunned when it easily slipped inside.

The sensation was new, erotic…unexpected, and it sent her over the edge. Her legs gave out as a orgasmic wave took hold. He pressed up against her, holding her up with his shoulders. She heard the *chink* of his belt hit the floor and a second later, he glided inside.

"You're so warm," he cooed in her ear.

Still tense from orgasm, his cock caressing her inside kept her nerves on edge. She gasped for air as she clutched his shoulders.

"So wet."

She had no words, only oxygen to try to capture as he drove into her. Why had she waited so long to experience this pleasure? She didn't have the answer, nor did she care. His walls came down and she felt herself around him and screamed out as her orgasm peaked.

Her orgasm had an effect on him as he drove into her and bit down on her shoulder. "Ugh, Nala!" he wailed.

Lifting her, he carried her to the bed. Once she was eased onto its surface, he was once again inside her. She fought to block him, the sensations he was feeling, because one more orgasm might render her completely incapacitated.

She pushed him off of her. He rolled to his back, look of longing and hunger in his eyes. She wanted to do something different, but her experience was lacking. She began to mount him when she decided to turn around. Crouching over him, with her back to him, she reached down to cup his balls as she eased herself onto his cock.

She heard him gasp and smiled.

If he was feeling carnal, she was going to give him carnal. Getting to her knees, she moved her ass up and down his cock, giving him a show while pleasuring him. Thinking she hand the upper hand she continued to move up and down on his cock, the new angle giving her a new sense of pleasure.

The feeling of his fingers, intruding the space startled her for a minute. Slick with the remnants of her orgasm, she felt a thumb or finger swirling around her ass again. She quickened her pace to distract him, unsure she was quite ready for that sort of play.

When his digit slid inside, and another finger swirled around her already sensitive clit, she nearly lost her mind and couldn't move. He did the work from below her, pushing in. She cried out in frustration and pleasure.

"Oh fuck!" he gasped.

Both hands slapped her ass cheeks then pulled her down on him hard as he came with his own orgasm.

He released her and she repositioned next to him. "Wow, what was that?"

After a gasp, a chuckle, and a moment to catch his breath he rolled to face her. "Our connection, I think. I just sort of knew you wanted to try a bit of anal play, but not too much. So I started off slow."

She felt the heat of embarrassment licking her face. "Not that, I mean…it was so different."

Gazing into her eyes, his brows furrowed briefly, then relaxed as he smiled. "I think that's our connection too. Just. Feeling how concerned you've been with my outcome. I mean," he paused for a moment, staring at the ceiling. Her heart thundered in her chest as she waited for him to speak. "Look, we had an arranged marriage. An actual business deal when you get down to it. Even in the midst of my tiptoeing around you because I knew what you came from, and your tiptoeing around me because I was in mourning and now dethroned—somehow, some way, we still managed to find mutual respect and concern for the well-being of our mate. That was before the bond. It's just…"

"It became a lot more clear after the bond?" she finished for him. "That night, when we bonded, the emotion I felt from you was a little overwhelming. Then, it was a shock, to have someone put my needs first. To have someone care for me, in the manner of non-romantic love." She squeezed her eyes shut tight then opened them. "I mean, the amount of admiration, respect, warmth you felt that had nothing to do with romance or mating. I felt all of that. It really changed how I look at you, how I think and feel."

He began to snicker.

"What?" she asked.

"Maybe we should have bonded that first night. It would have saved us some trouble."

She couldn't help but agree with him, or at least his sense of humor. "Yes, but the way we did it…the way *you* did it. That was beautiful."

Wrapping his arms around her, he pulled her in tight, holding his lips to her forehead for a moment. In a low voice he whispered, "Like I said, you're not alone anymore. I get you. I get it. I'm here."

She felt the smile spread across her lips. "Same here. You're not alone."

"Let's keep it that way."

NINE

The following morning during her normal workout routine, Nala had reached her favorite tree with her favorite branch. It was a typical Tennessee morning, sunny and humid. Rays of light pierced through the canopy of trees, licking the forest floor. She pulled herself up, inhaling as she did so. The smell of the earth, damp forest floor and the lush greenery surrounding her, danced in her nostrils. Blowing the air out as she extended her arms, she could still smell the moss and dirt. She inhaled again as she lifted her chin above the branch. This time, another smell…something foreign…something living.

She dropped to the dirt below her and scanned the area, testing the air again. The familiar pinching between her blades made her stomach leap. A Lycan was near, and it wasn't a pack member. Sniffing again, she made a mental note of the smell…but couldn't identify it. It was musty, like an old basement.

Crack! The sound of a breaking twig caused her to snap her head the left, just in time to see the wolf, crouching low in the stalking position. Its dark grey fur failed to shine in the sunlight. There were two more behind him, one brown, and one sandy in color.

Security Breach! She screamed out in her head to her mate, praying their connection would reach him. With a deep cleansing breath, she fought to remain calm. Footsteps to her right pulled her attention to Stephany Kincade strolling toward her, a large male wolf trailing behind.

"Hello there."

She crossed her arms over her chest. "Come for a workout, Stephany?" Her heart thundered. She was now outnumbered five to one. She might be tough, but those were unfavorable odds.

"You disrespected me," she snapped.

"You disrespected *and* attacked a pack member. My response was measured and warranted." She lifted her chin, asserting herself as an Alpha. "It's my duty to protect my pack."

"Where are you?" Colin's panicked voice came through, reassuring her.

My workout trail, by the tree. Hurry!

"That Alpha shit might work with your pack. But to me, you're nothing more than another bitch in my way. I've brought some of my friends to teach you a lesson in respect."

The three wolves started approaching from the left as Stephany and her companion approached from the right. She had two choices, fight or run. She couldn't survive an attack of four wolves and a scorned female. Running was the safest option, but she didn't want to give Stephany the satisfaction.

Taking a few steps back, she shifted her eyes back and forth. "I figured you for a coward. It gives me great solace knowing I was right."

Howls and screams from the left startled Nala until she saw that five Gnomes were going crazy, vibrating like Mary had, on the three wolves there. They clawed and stabbed at the wolves eyes.

Two Lycans…two she could handle.

Stephany charged her.

Nala swung her open hand, connecting with Stephany's cheek, slapping her in the face to add insult to injury. "Down girl!" She growled at her.

The wolf behind Stephany lunged at Nala but was stopped in midair by a Centaur hoof. To Nala's shock and amazement, Prometheus had joined the rescue squad. The wolf shifted to heal what was certainly an injured rump.

"Jackson!" Stephany squealed as she ran over to her mate.

"What is the meaning of this ambush?" Nala's screamed at the top of her lungs. All commotion stopped.

Jackson stood from the ground and limped toward her. "You disrespected my mate! You have to pay for that!"

Turning slightly away from him so as to brace herself for a fight, she growled. "This is not the proper means to settle a dispute and you *know* that. There are customs. There are laws! This was a cowardly attack. Five to one? Are you all such sniveling, cowardly weaklings?"

Prometheus stepped between them. "I'm reporting your actions to FOSE. For now, you are trespassing and must leave." He looked down on the Lycan. "Unless of course you'd like to continue? I'm certain you won't since you lost your significant advantage."

"I issue a challenge!" Spittle flew from his mouth as he screamed. Veins bulged in his neck.

Nala's heart stopped.

"One week from today," he spat. "Scottsboro land."

Shaking her head, she refused. "I won't step foot on Scottsboro ground. If you want a challenge, you'll do it here, on the land you're trying to confiscate. You'll do it by the book. That means no more trespassing, no more ambushes by you, your people, or any proxy." She stuck out her hand. "Order it now and it's done. You *are* the pack's Beta, are you not?"

His low growl and scowl didn't scare her. He finally took

her hand and shook it, but only for a split second.

"I order you all to stand down. No one is to come to Belfast until a week from today by my order." His announcement made Stephany seethe.

She stormed over pointing her finger at Nala. "Make your funeral arrangements now. You're one dead were-bitch!"

Colin ran up behind Nala. When she turned to look at him, she was shocked to see him so disheveled. His shirt was torn and he had blood dripping from his nose.

"I have a message for you from your brother." He looked at Stephany, his smile wide. "He abjures you."

It might have been the only time Nala would witness emotion in the eyes of her nemesis. The words had wounded her as evidenced by the large tears gathering in her eyes.

"Get off my land," Nala barked at them before turning on her heel. "What happened to you?"

"Jake. Jake wanted me to let you handle this without me. We fought." He threw his arms around her and pulled her in tight. "Damn I was so worried."

"I'll escort them to the property line," Prometheus offered with a slight bow of his head toward her.

Having a Centaur warrior escort them made a clear statement. "Thank you."

"You look like hell. Did you two really fight?"

He laughed as his head bobbed. "He's strong as a bear, I tell you. You don't have to ever worry about him losing a battle. He'd rip his own arm off to beat you with it if he had to. My brother is crazy."

As they made their way back toward the house, he described their fight in detail. It was less of a fight and more like Jake restraining Colin, insisting that Nala had to prove herself as Alpha. "He said that if I came to your rescue it would undermine you as Alpha."

"It would, except it was an ambush."

"That's what I tried to tell him. But the others were on

their way already and…let's just say that we disagreed…strongly."

She spoke in a low voice so the others following could not hear. "I've never heard of abjure. What does that mean?"

He turned his head to look her in the eye. The look was sad. "It's how you disown your family permanently. It's a very old tradition not used much anymore but it's as formal as it comes—and permanent."

"Did he really do that? When? Were you on the phone with him?" When they reached the house, Nala took a seat on the patio, pulling her mate next to her as she examined his nose.

"When you called out to me, Roman and Grace heard you. He sent the message telepathically." He waved her hand away from his face. "My nose is fine. I healed already."

"I don't understand," she said as she leaned back against the table, "why didn't he tell me?"

His hand was wrapped around hers in an instant. "We sort of all talked about this when you became Alpha. We knew you'd face adversity and that your strength, both inner strength and perceived strength would come from your dealing with that adversity. We don't want the others thinking you need our rescue to be Alpha, just as when I was Alpha." He rubbed his face. "Since I was the Alpha of this pack, it is very important it doesn't appear I'm a defacto-alpha. You earned your spot. It's not a façade."

As she fought to digest what he said, anger welled up inside. How was it that everyone was privy to this discussion except the woman in question?

"Because, it's more effective when you're allowed to act and make decisions without the outside influence of that knowledge." His unexpected wink chilled the fire flowing through her veins. How could she continually forget he could now hear her thoughts?

"I see."

"You just faced your first challenge head-on, without

fear or hesitance. You did that because I wasn't lurking. Jake was right to hold me back." Large heavy arms wrapped around her as he pulled her in for another hug. "Bastards. Five-on-one? Who does that?"

With a deep cleansing breath, she leaned back against the stone table. She closed her eyes for a moment, forcing herself to calm. "I saw this coming. I knew when I protected a Gnome and restrained her she'd get revenge. It isn't hard to see her moral compass does exactly point due North."

Colin shook his head. "She's always been different. Stephany never fit in here, which is why she migrated to Chicago. She wanted to be by the big city, not among the *dirty* forest. Roman suspects they have different fathers, though never had any real reason to think his mother was unfaithful."

"What?" She shook her head. "Weren't his parents bonded?"

He shrugged, his lips sagged into a frown. "It was an arranged marriage. They never went through with the bond."

"So why was the Centaur here?" She posed the question to give her mind time to catch up. Stephany might have a different father than Roman…and she never really fit in. Now she's money and power hungry. It could explain her motivations.

"Because I get to see you in a dress." His laugh was quiet as his brow wagged at her.

"Excuse me?"

"Well, he came with wedding invitations. So I get to see you in a dress again."

Her heart fell in her shoes. She didn't have a dress, nor was she comfortable wearing dress shoes now that she had to watch her back even more. "I see. Who is getting married?"

"Hey!" He nudged her. "I felt that. Why so glum? It just gives us another excuse to take a trip into town."

When his hand reached her thigh, the soothing warmth

of his palm eased her off her internal ledge. "You still haven't told me who is getting married."

"Ah, yes. Wendy's little Gnome friend, Mary. The Gnomes are so excited they wanted to invite nearly everyone. You are among the most wanted because you were the first Lycan Alpha to invite them to integrate. We have special seats and everything."

Oh good, easy targets.

"Hey," he whispered in her ear, "you're really shaken up by this. I get that, but you'll be surrounded by dozens of warriors. Relax. It's a party." His gentle kiss pressed against her temple momentarily and once again, she felt her nerves ease up.

"But I have been challenged, Colin. How am I supposed to celebrate when I'm so worried?" She scrubbed her face with her hand. "I can't even exercise without fear of another ambush. Don't think for one second I took that mutt for his word."

The clacking of hooves approached. Prometheus wore a serious scowl that did little to keep Nala calm. "The heathens are gone, Nala. But I must warn you, they're concocting some plan. I overheard the thoughts of the female. She clamped up before I caught it. But I heard her think something about a surprise for us all."

She stood and brushed her hands on her pants. "We're already on high alert here. We know who we're dealing with."

The air shimmered briefly as he shifted to human form. "If I may...give you some advice?"

"Advice? Sure."

"Your aura reads of self-doubt. You must believe in yourself, Lycan warrior. You are a true Alpha. If you go into battle assuming he's stronger and more skilled, you *will* lose. You must cleanse yourself."

"That's reassuring."

"Nala, just listen to him," Colin begged.

Prometheus continued. "If you can remove the doubt,

your will be clear headed and have a full advantage. You've fought and won. You have taken on three Lycans...and won. You defeated a brutal ruler while in a weakened state. This Jackson fellow will be a challenge, but you *will* win. You *must* believe that. In two hundred years I've not met a female of your caliber. Also in that two hundred years, I've never met a Lycan more determined, more concerned that you, ma'am. That's two centuries of experience I have to offer." He cleared his throat. "Now, to a more tender subject...I'd like to offer a few of our men for extra security."

"Absolutely not! You leave them at that school to protect those kids!" Her voice boomed through the air, startling Colin and Prometheus.

"As you wish." His lips spread wide, his teeth gleaming as he smiled. "Pure of heart as well. Yes, a true warrior. You'll walk through the heathen if you believe in yourself."

"Training starts now!" A voice came from behind her as large hands pushed hard on her back and a foot looped around her ankles. She hit the dirt, face first.

"What the hell?" Colin screamed.

"Stay back if you love your mate," Prometheus ordered with a finger pointed at Colin.

Tom, head of security, jumped on her back, pulling at her wrist. Nala bucked, knocking him off her back as she scrambled to her feet. She shifted to wolf at growled. Tom wasted no time shifting and lunged at her once again, grabbing her by the back of the neck and flipping her in the air. Twisting, she managed to land on her feet running as she charged him.

Something hard crunched against her ribs and sending her flying to the right. The Centaur had transformed and kicked her with a hoof.

"You must be prepared for anything. Keep focused. They might take a formal challenge and use it as an ambush." Prometheus stood high on his horse body. "Move your eyes constantly. Keep aware."

Still sore from the last rib breaking, she noticed that

healing had already begun as a normal Lycan should. The poison had left her body. For the first time, she had hope.

Tom lunged at her once more, this time taking a bite out of her front and hind quarter as he passed. She yelped at the searing pain in her wound.

"I can't watch," Colin yelled as he ran into the house.

Fighting to ignore the pain in her mate's voice, she looked back and forth between Prometheus and Tom. Who would attack first?

"Don't play defense. Take the offense!" The Centaur yelled at her.

She stalked around Tom. He moved to keep his muzzle and body pointed toward her. She took a mental note of it. She faked to the right before darting left, grabbing his leg with her teeth and yanking, which dropped him to the ground. She bit at this shoulder first, then his hind leg. As he scrambled and yelped, she took another bite at the back of his neck.

This time, she kept an eye on the Centaur. When a hoof came at her, she jumped out of the way and bit at it, scraping it with her teeth before taking another swipe at Tom.

"Excuse me!" Jake yelled. "Chances are, there won't be a Centaur on their side. Let's make this as real as it comes."

Prometheus stepped back as Jake shifted and headed for Nala. Growling and snarling like a true opponent.

Her head dropped below her shoulders as her heart sank. She was now going to have to attack her brother-in-law. As he approached, she crouched down to give herself better leverage and leaped. Pain shot through her core as her chest collided with his shoulder. Jake fell over and yelped before scrambling to his feet. When Nala attempted the same move, he grabbed the back of her neck and jerked hard. She felt fire where his teeth pierced her coat. He wasn't taking it easy on her.

"Stop thinking like a wolf. Fight! Use all of your resources!" Prometheus ordered.

Nala and Jake stopped at looked at him. Tom shifted.

"That's not how Lycans fight."

"You don't think that man is going to cheat? Really? Because that whole pack is as filthy as it gets." The Centaur crossed his arms over his chest.

She paused and looked around. When Tom shifted, he ran at her to attack once more. She waited…watched…until he was a foot away, and then shifted, grabbing a stick and stabbing him in the shoulder.

"Yes!" Prometheus cheered. "That's it. Again!"

Now lying on the ground in human form, Tom pulled the stick out of his shoulder. "That fucking hurt. Do it again!"

When Jake lunged at her, she chose a rock and bashed him in the head.

Tom's final attack broke her jaw as his fist connected. She fought back the tears as blinding pain radiated through her face. When she shifted back, the Centaur walked over to her. "It's just dislocated. Hang on…this is going to hurt." With more unbelievable pain, he pushed her jaw back into place.

"Ugh," she groaned, fighting back the real tears of pain that were lingering beneath the surface.

"Don't sweat it, Warrior…I doubt your opponent is going to be this skilled. Keep practicing. Stop three days before battle. It'll give you enough time to heal fully and anticipate the fight." Prometheus pounded his chest twice before heading into the house.

Nala plopped down on the bench. Jake sat next to her. "Damn, you're tough as nails. I'm very impressed. If we weren't pack mates, Tom and I would be dead."

"Speaking of training, no more morning working out alone. We will train every morning." Tom bowed slightly and headed down the path toward the security shack that now housed the monitors.

"Jake, make sure you don't take it easy on me." Leaning forward, she rested her elbows on her knees. "If I'm going to survive a challenge from an Alpha or a Beta male, I need you to give me all you've got." *And I'll do my best not to kill you out of instinct.*

"We won't kill a pack mate. Relax." Her wolf's reassurance did little to calm her worry.

He huffed. "Are you kidding me? I *was* giving it all I had. I hit and bit as hard as I could. Nala, really, you're going to plow through that douchebag." Standing, he offered a hand to help her off the bench. She gladly took it. "You'd better go see my brother. That was hard on him."

"Yeah, thanks for everything. I chose my Beta wisely." She winked and spun on her heel toward the house. The smell of breakfast hit her hard, causing her stomach to growl. As she entered the dining room, she found Colin staring at a plate of yet-to-be-touched breakfast.

"You okay?" he asked as she pulled out her chair.

"I was about to ask you the same question."

"That was awful. But I swear on our bond that I won't run when the actual challenge happens. I'll stay and will you to win." A weak smile spread across his face. "Lycan's honor."

Breakfast went down quickly. The soreness had subsided by the time she hit the shower. She thanked her Lycan genes for the quick recovery and ridding her body of whatever toxin had slowed the healing until now.

Colin had taken the training hard. Having a large Centaur and the head of security both attack her at once had been too much. How would he react if she lost her life in the challenge? She cursed their bond yet again, and the very real risk to her mate's heart.

"It's my risk to take," his voice was low as he opened the shower door. "I know what I've gotten myself into, Nala." Stepping in, he closed the door behind him. "I have faith in you, just not Stephany's mate. He's as dirty as they come, I can just feel it."

She wrapped arms around his neck. "I love you. I am sorry that you constantly have to worry about me."

"We get to celebrate at a wedding this weekend. Two days later, you're going to be fighting for your life and the wellbeing of our pack. I want you to promise me you'll eat as much as you can. Get as much rest as possible. Let Jake handle the business end of the pack this week. You need your strength." His arms closed around her back and squeezed her. "Do those things for me. The challenge is what it is. We knew it would come."

Resting her sopping wet head on his shoulder, she closed her eyes, allowing herself to relax. "I will win."

"Yes. You will." Soothing hands stroked her back as the hot shower poured over them. "Until then, we're going to train, shop, and celebrate."

When she lifted her head, his lips met hers in an instant. Knotting her fingers in his hair, she pulled him in harder, her heart leaping with the sudden excitement that had taken the place of fear. Her mate believed in her as did key members of her pack. A Centaur had admired her skills and her heart. She had to remove her trepidation and practice faith once again.

Teeth lightly bit at her neck, sending flames of need to her core. His hands slid down to her thighs and he lifted her up while stepping toward the stone shower wall. After gently easing her back against the hard surface, he positioned himself at her opening. Their eyes locked as he eased her down on his cock.

A small gasp released as her body accommodated him. Small jets of water tickled her nipples which stood at attention. His head fell forward and rested at her collarbone as he thrust into her again. He lifted his head, kissing her once more. The kiss held urgency and passion like she hadn't experienced before. As he devoured her mouth, his cock filled her to her core.

Gone was the need to be so delicate. With their bond, he could sense exactly what she felt and aggression rocked her mind. After easing her feet to the floor, he turned off the water and exited the shower, pulling her with him. He dropped a towel on the floor before the sink and positioned her wet feet on it, shoulder width apart. Strong hands made their way down her arms, until they held her wrists and planted them on the counter.

Their image reflected in the mirror made her heart race even more, both sopping wet, cheeks flushed. He guided himself in from behind, impaling her once more. Rough hands made their way to her hips, holding her firm as he thrust into her.

"Look at me!" she cried out.

He looked at her in the mirror, eyes illuminated in their beautiful golden glow. A low growl rumbled in his throat and he squeezed her hips, picking up the pace. Her heart raced as he pounded into her from behind, exhilarated at the pace…at his need. His right hand released her hip and quickly fisted in her hair, forcing her head to turn so that he could devour her lips once more.

She moaned into the kiss, which sent her mate wild. After lightly biting her bottom lip, he clenched his jaw, thrusting into her a final time before pulling out and spilling his seed on the towel. Still breathing hard, he spun her around and kicked her feet apart. A gentle push on her shoulders had her leaning back on the counter before he commenced in kissing and licking her neck. He trailed down to her breasts, gently sucking on her nipple. A firm hand between her legs massaged her nerve bundle, making her whimper. Keeping his thumb on her clit, he slid two fingers inside. As the delicious sensation buzzed within her, she panted. Her knees, threatened to buckle as the blood rushed to her core, which quivered at the precipice.

His loving fingers massaged her to the crest as her orgasm swept over her. She cried out as she rode the wave of ecstasy.

"That's it, love." He kissed her neck.

"Wow," she gasped. Her shaky legs revolted against her as she stood upright.

"Indeed." He winked then stepped away, turning the shower on.

After a good rinse, she toweled off and headed for the

bed. Colin soon followed.

"Every time I curse this bond; you're going to remind me of its benefits, aren't you?" She chuckled realizing how phenomenal the bond made the sex.

"If I have to keep you in perpetual orgasm, it's a sacrifice I'm willing to make."

She turned to see a large smile on his face. "Oh, the horror!"

Laugher echoed in their room. She pushed back thoughts of the challenge. There was no way on earth she was going to spoil the post-coital bliss, but the thought of that damned note crept in.

"What note?" Colin asked.

With a sigh, she rolled over and opened her night stand drawer, pulled out the note and handed it to Colin.

"Enemies within our pack, Colin." She closed her eyes, wishing it all away.

TEN

Against her better judgment, she allowed Colin to give the note to Jake who was enraged at the message.

"I'll get down to the bottom of this. Mark my words!" Jake roared and slammed his fist on his desk. "For now, don't worry about this. Train and prepare. Let me handle this nonsense."

While it was quite possibly the best course of action, she hated that it made her feel weak, needing the men around her to watch over her. This was one of many times she'd question her choice to be Alpha. It wasn't that she didn't understand the risks, the responsibility...but the amount of enemies she'd acquire had far surpassed her expectation.

Dinner in their room was followed by two rounds of vivacious lovemaking that kept Nala in a state of euphoria she wished would last forever.

The next three days followed the same pattern of training, breakfast, showering, followed by lovemaking, lunch and numerous other distractions. Colin had succeeded in the distraction department with two trips searching for a dress for Nala to wear to the wedding. While she only concerned herself with mobility in the event she'd have to defend herself, Colin argued for a more form fitting cocktail dress. They'd met in the middle with a thigh length black dress that flowed once past her waist with a formfitting lace bodice on top.

She was once again in her bathroom, on a stool, while Carissa, the pack beautician, worked her magic. Her dark hair had been pulled into an elegant French twist, accentuated with baby blue gems along both sides. Carissa had insisted on a bit more makeup since it was an evening event.

"What are those?" Nala pointed at the black, caterpillar like things on the beautician's finger.

"Fake eyelashes. Hold still."

"Nope! No way. Get those things away from me. My eyelashes are fine."

With a sigh, she tossed them in the trash. "Really, it would have been so beautiful."

She snickered. "I already let you put three extra layers of makeup on me. I think I've given as much as I'm willing."

"Well, let's see what you think." Carissa stepped back and held her arm out toward the mirror.

Nala stood from her stool and looked at her reflection. She had to hand it to the crazy Lycan beautician. The extra makeup had given her a magical transformation.

"Stunning. Right?"

She shook her head. "I wouldn't go that far."

"Ha!" She tossed her brushes in her bag. "You could be on the cover of Vogue. Who are you kidding? With that bone structure and skin tone…it was the perfect canvas."

Pulling the tissue from around the neck of her dress, which plunged too low for her liking, she had a view of the full deal. It would be impossible for her not to feel sexy like this. The low neck line made her feel less a warrior and more a harlot, but it had given her mate an erection he couldn't hide in the store. It seemed like the perfect torture device for him, so she conceded.

"Enjoy the wedding!" Carissa called over her shoulder as she hurried out of the bathroom.

She continued to stare at herself in disbelief. *Makeup is amazing.*

"Not that you need it." Colin's voice came from behind her. When she turned she saw his face slightly red.

"I might need to wear an extra pair of underwear tonight. Damn you look sexy."

Heat radiated around her neck and licked at her cheeks. "Thank you." She wagged her finger for him to step from behind the door, which he was using to conceal himself.

When he stepped out, she saw his tuxedo. "Wow, you clean up nice!" Teasing with a wink, she smacked his behind as she passed him. "I just have to slip on my shoes."

"Wait!" The smile on his face was wide before he darted into his closet. She sat on the bed, curious as to what he could be up to.

He returned with a shoe box. "I had these especially made for you."

When he opened the box, back heels stared back at her. "I don't understand."

"Well," he said taking a knee by her feet, "my little warrior Alpha has been so worried about defending herself, I had them reinforce this section with steel." He pointed to the photo inside the lid. "This is what they can transform into—a steel toed shoe so you can kick someone's ass if you need to."

Moisture in her eyes threatened to ruin Carissa's handiwork. "This is oddly the sweetest thing you could have done."

When she slid her feet into them, she could feel the stiffness from the steel. It made her feel near giddy. "So when I shift, I can shift the shoes into those?"

His head bobbed as his smile widened. "Yep."

"Fantastic!" She quickly stood from the bed, walked a few paces and held out her hand. "Let's go party."

Once in the car, Nala did the best she could to quiet her mind and think of anything but the upcoming challenge against Jackson Kincade.

"Can I ask a silly question?"

Colin's grip on the wheel tightened as he glanced at her. "I doubt it's silly, but you can ask me anything."

"When you said you did what you could to quiet your mind so I wouldn't be inundated with your thoughts, how'd you do it?" She balled her hands in her lap, embarrassed she didn't know the answer already.

"Ah yes, my mother taught me that little trick. See, my father was Alpha. Mom was a worrier. She'd have to occupy her mind so as not to distract him with her worrying. What she told me was to visualize something that makes you feel calm and relaxed. For me, that's sitting by the water, sun warming my body, frogs in the background. What makes you feel calm and relaxed?"

She looked down at her hands and clamed up.

"Nala?"

She cleared the lump out of her throat. "When I was little I had a hard time sleeping. I was sort of wired all of the time. My mother used to lay in bed behind me and stroke my hair." A soft laugh escaped. "I swear her fingers were like magic. I'd start off feeling like I wanted to go run and play. Before I knew it, my eyes would start to feel heavy. My muscles would relax and I would just pass out." She took a deep cleansing breath, ridding herself of the loss she was feeling all over again. "It was the safest place in the world, lying in front of her."

"Then think of that when you feel overwhelmed and trust me when I tell you that the more you think of it, the less you'll feel like crying. I promise."

She closed her eyes and let the memories of her mother flood her mind. She'd been so quiet...so passive. Her mother silently raised a strong, independent, Lycan woman. No one would have thought her mother to be the sort that filled her head with thoughts of Alpha-ship someday.

"Wow!" Colin's voice caused her eyes to pop open. The long drive had been lit by torches that led to numerous large tents which were lit with small lanterns.

"So this is their tradition, huh? Nice."

"Actually, no. But according to Wendy, they wanted to have it during the evening so Gustav and a few other vampires could attend. I think the Gnomes are probably the most attuned to integration. They really do try to get along with everyone."

Nala couldn't agree more. They even gave gifts to their enemy.

After they parked the car, they made their way to the tented area, which was swarming with supernaturals of all kinds. The atmosphere was charged with elation, a welcomed feeling for Nala, and from what she could feel coming from him, Colin.

"I'm so glad you came!" Mary shuffled over in her dress. Wendy had hand sewn the little gown, attaching countless tiny pearls. Her curly brown hair was wound into a braided crown. Adorable and excited, the little woman bounced up and down.

"You look lovely." Nala sat in the nearest chair and leaned down. "Congratulations on your wedding day."

With her hands clutched to the skirt of her wedding gown, the little woman twirled. "Isn't it lovely? Wendy made it for me. She's such a good friend!" A squeal came from her as her smile widened. "Oh look, it's almost time. Grab your seats over there. We're doing this here, where the reception is."

Before Nala could reply, Mary ran off toward a group of Gnomes standing at the front of the tent. Nala took Colin's hand and walked to their seats.

"Xander! It's good to see you," Colin said as he threw his arms around him.

"Thank you. It's good to see you as well. Nala." He nodded at her. "I think we're about to start."

Grace, Roman, Wendy, and Zoltar joined them at the special table reserved just for them.

An elder Gnome hobbled to a tiny podium and called attention. "Since the beginning of our recorded history, a

Gnome wedding was no more than the parents declaring their offspring as a couple. This assumed, of course, that the parents were still alive and happy with the union. As we supernatural beings have moved to a more civilized way of life, our people have discussed the forming of unions in a more formal manner. Mary and Bart have asked us to manage their wedding in a certain way, but you're all free to have whatever ceremony you wish."

All of the little heads in the enormous tent bobbed. The Elder continued.

"Life is delicate, this much we all know. Some of us live much longer than others, but in the grand picture, our time here is but a blink of an eye. In that tiny fraction of a moment in time, we have a limited amount of days, hours, minutes, and even seconds to make each moment count; to make every life matter, every friendship, and every courtship must matter to the fullest extent allowable. In the last year, Mary has blossomed among our kind. She was the first to step up and speak for us, the first to run with the Lycans, the first to befriend with another species. Our Mary has risked her life for her friends, has spilled blood to protect those she has cherished, and while taking a life is no small matter, she has done so with honorable intention. She's fierce, charitable, and loyal to her fullest. Her closest friend is a Lycan, Wendy Baker. With Wendy's help, Mary established the first Gnome settlement among the Lycan's of Nala Baker's clan."

Applause erupted through the tent.

"Together with the Centaur King, Zoltar, Mary worked though she was exhausted and drained, to establish a feasible mode of transportation for our kind." He nodded to Zoltar, who smiled and bobbed his head in return.

"So when Mary looked to a mate, she looked toward Bart, who proudly holds a seat at FOSE headquarters. Bart also was chosen by the Fae as a member of the Special Opps unit tasked with tracking down those who mean to do us harm. This special member of our society worked tirelessly on the erection of this very school, working to uniting us all. Mary looked for a special mate among our people and found Bart to be her match. Together, they represent all that we are and all that we will be as we move forward."

Another round of applause filled the air as Mary and Bart joined hands.

"Mary," the elder started as he rapped ivy around her wrist, "you are now joined to Bart, bound until death. Do you wish it so?"

"I wish it very much." She sniffed.

He continued binding their wrists together with the ivy. "Bart, you are now joined to Mary, bound until death. Do you wish it so?"

"It's my honor."

"Then the Great Mother binds you until death. You may kiss."

As their lips joined, everyone stood from their chairs, clapping, whistling, and congratulating the couple. Nala's heart swelled to bursting as Colin's emotions blended with her own. When she felt his hand around her wrist, she turned to face him. Before she could react, his lips met hers in a swift kiss.

"I couldn't help myself," he said with a grin.

Her lips tightened as she fought to hide a smile. "I don't blame you. What a beautiful speech."

"Yes, you are beautiful." Twisting her words, he wagged his brows at her.

Champagne was poured and Wendy toasted the couple. "Now, two dozen of our students have volunteered to serve us tonight. Please be gracious and watch the language." She turned to Zoltar. "Because some of us get a little wicked when tipsy."

The students came in carrying plates full of food, delivering them to the guests. A blonde dropped Nala's plate hard on the table in front of her. "Enjoy," she huffed.

"Geeze, don't volunteer unless you want to be nice," she grumbled under her breath. The moment the words escaped her lips, she felt a twinge between her shoulder blades. The tiny hairs stood up on the back of her neck.

"Colin…"

Movement in the tent halted as everyone's senses were on edge. Something had happened, but she couldn't put her finger on it.

"Call all of your men," Beauregard said to Zoltar. "Everyone on Guard!"

The thundering of hooves could be heard as the Centaur herd approached. Nala quickly stood from the table. She back away as the air around her shimmered and she shifted into wolf.

Screams could be heard in the distance. They were female. Two Centaurs ran in the direction of the screams.

Kaboom! The sky lit as some sort of bomb hit an invisible shield. Nala couldn't quite understand what she was seeing. *Crack! Kaboom!* More explosions erupted high in the sky. Was this part of the celebration?

"No, it's not!" Wendy shuffled around to the other side of Nala.

The two dozen servants came running back toward the tent, many of them wielding swords taken from armor displays in the castle. Nala was thankful they came to join in the defense. They might be young, but numbers mattered in battle.

Her feelings changed in a split second as one of the blades came down, cutting the Elder Gnome in two. A Fae shot a ball of light from his hands, hitting the boy in the chest. The sword flew out of his hands and was caught by a Dwarf who charged the students.

"It's mayhem! Fuck!" Zoltar shifted and took off toward the crowd.

Nala froze for a moment, unable to tell who was friend and who was foe.

"Focus on who is attacking whom. Use your best judgement." Colin's voice came through as he ran toward the fight.

Nala crouched down and sprang over the table, stopping

next to Mary. *No one should die on their wedding day.* She climbed on Nala's back. "Get them! Kill them all!" She screamed.

She tore off toward the fighting, grabbing a Werepanther who was clawing at a Pixie who was doing her best to fend off the attacker. Once she had her teeth in the panther's neck, she pulled hard, rolling it away from the Pixie. Quick to its feet, the Panther swiped at her, cutting her snout. As the heat of the gash seared through her snout, she circled the animal. A new opponent would be good for her training.

The cat leaped at her, Nala shifted right before the cat made contact and kicked it hard with her steel toe shoe. She felt the ribs crack under her foot. She rolled again, grabbing a serving knife she spotted and plunging it into the cat's side.

It let out a blood curdling howl.

The thundering of paws came from her left. She looked in time to see a young Lycan charging her and shifted to wolf, taking a chunk of panther throat with her as she turned to her new opponent. She sniffed the Lycan as she dodged his charge. They immediately shifted. "Xander, it's me!" She screamed.

He stopped, his muzzle dropping open.

"Don't worry about it. Go!"

She looked around for Mary, wondering what happened to her during the fight. High pitched growling came from behind her, so she spun around. Mary was mounted on a bear's head, clawing at its eyes. She was vibrating, her eyes wide and blood red.

Nala shifted back to wolf. She'd never taken on a bear, but it was blind now. She ran to it, grabbing a mouthful of its leg and bit down, ripping a chunk off the animal. It roared in response.

"I'm coming! I'm coming!" Grace's voice screamed in her head. She could see the enormous wolf approaching. *"Together, on three. One…two…three!"*

Grace grabbed the left wrist and Nala followed suit grabbing the right. They both pulled with everything they had, but Grace's size gave her a lot more strength.

Another Lycan snout appeared next to Nala's. She turned her eyes to see Xander pulling with her. Relieved he was okay and fighting with her, she pulled with everything she could, clamping her canines down on the wrist of the bear. Warm metallic blood flowed into her mouth.

When the bear's left arm became detached, he howled out in pain, bent forward, and locked his jaws on Xander's head. She could hear the crunching and grinding of bone and saw Xander's eyes roll. Grace mounted the bear's back and bit down on his neck. Warm red covered Nala's face. She blinked to clear her vision, and finally shifted back to human form.

"Xander! No!" She knelt down next to him. "It's going to be okay. Shift. Can you hear me? Shift now!"

He flopped on the ground. Gurgling sounds came from his mouth.

"Grace!" she cried.

Grace laid her hands on him and forced him to shift, which did little to heal his wounds. His head was split open and blood was leaking out. Around them people were still fighting and whatever blasts that started, continued but now grew closer.

"Grace!" Nala laid her hands on Xander. "Oh the gods, no!"

A tall man dropped to his knees on the other side of Xander. His hands hovered over his head. "Go!" He looked at Nala and Grace. "Go! I will take care of him."

She looked at Grace, her stomach in knots. "The one who served me…I think she's from my old pack. She smelled familiar."

Nala shifted back to wolf, rage boiling in her veins. Jagger had come back to haunt her. He wasn't going to win. Not again. Her eyes scanned the area and she found two humans with large tubes on their shoulders. One of the tubes erupted sending a ball of fire toward them. Her eyes narrowed and she launched herself straight at them. Fiery tubes or not, she was going to *end* them.

The sound of galloping followed her. She didn't turn to see who it was. Instead, she dug in, running harder and faster than she ever had. A tingle of electricity raced through her.

"That's the protective spell we passed," Theron, Zoltar's second in command said as he approached her flank. "We're unprotected out here. Watch your back." He drew back his arrow and released it, hitting one of the humans in the knee.

She wanted to ask why humans were now attacking them. What had they ever done to the humans except stay out of their way?

As she came to the top of the hill, she saw thirty or more humans behind the ones with the fiery tubes. *Shit! Colin, Grace, Zoltar…whomever, we've got trouble!"*

Gustav appeared out of thin air next to one of the tube holders and bit his neck, bit his own finger and crammed it in the guy's mouth. He did the same with every man holding the large metal tubes. Almost immediately, they fell to the ground.

"Stop!" He shouted to the humans. "Why are you attacking this school? I demand to know!"

The humans started screaming and holding up crosses. Some were made of wood and some of metal.

Nala scanned the crowd, taking mental note of each face. She sniffed the air and all she could smell was fear and sulfur. She shifted to human.

"He asked you a question. I can smell your fear, but *you're* here attacking *us*. Not the other way around."

Before anyone could say or do anything, the vampire grabbed one of the men he'd bitten and looked into his eyes. Something must have given him the power to read their minds.

"Fools!" He shot up like a rod. "You're here trying to kill peaceful beings that have existed since the beginning of time. We've stayed hidden. We've stayed out of your way while you whore out the land, pollute everything you touch and breed like fucking rabbits and *you're* afraid of *us?*" He spat blood on the ground.

A woman stepped up, clutching a black leather book to her chest. "Demons!"

Gustav's laughter was eerie. "I could summon some if you'd like."

Nala shivered, but thought his approach didn't seem to work. Theron stood next to him with his bow pulled back ready to shoot anyone that stepped out of line.

"We saw you, on the internet, raping women…eating babies!" Her voice was shrill, terror licking at every word.

Zoltar, Roman, Wendy, and Grace approached. The humans eyes shifted and many of them took a step back.

Grace, they're terrified. They've seen the faked videos and they think we're monsters.

Wendy spoke first. "Those videos are faked. They are designed to scare you. We don't rape humans or eat babies. We eat the same things you do."

Grace walked forward until she was toe-to-toe with the woman clutching the book. "I grew up human and I can assure you, we are not evil. Nothing in that book covers what goes on here at this school. Your bible will neither guide nor protect you from any of it."

"Blasphemy!" she screeched.

"I didn't say God doesn't exist. What I'm saying is the Catholic Church edited the book at its inception to ensure supernaturals didn't taint your blood or your beliefs. That is all." She cleared her throat and stepped back, giving the woman a little breathing room.

The woman looked down at her book before clutching it to her chest. "I'll keep it if it's all the same to you."

Nala knew the situation could continue to get worse, or someone could make a move toward peace. She already had to worry about challengers to her seat, but now, the humans…they were out for blood. "You have no idea what you've done. How many people are hurt and scared."

Zoltar crossed his arms over his chest. "They're lucky

my pregnant wife is okay. Let's show them."

"Excuse me?" The bible clincher said.

Grace looked at him briefly then gave an affirmative nod. "That's a great idea. Instead of us all killing each other, why don't you come inside? You can see other than the wounded from your attack, our community is one of peace, of learning, and integration."

A man shouted from the back. "What's that gonna prove?"

Nala clenched her jaw in disbelief and anger. "You're willing to kill us, but not take a look around?"

Grace continued as if there was no question of a tour. "Now, if you'll all follow me, you can come meet the woman whose wedding you just destroyed and many more of our kind. You can take a tour of the school to see nothing sinister is taking place. Or…if you're more comfortable, you can *make an appointment* to take a *peaceful* tour of the school."

The woman backed away slowly. "You'll slaughter us."

"If you attack anyone, yes, you'll die. However if you peacefully proceed, not one hair will be harmed on any of your human heads. See, I am the Queen of the Lycans, or…as you know them, werewolves. This," she said pointing to Zoltar and Wendy, "is the King and Queen of the Centaurs. The other royals have assured me they've told their people to stand down so we can find a peaceful resolution to this conflict."

Nala looked around the humans, waiting for something to happen. Finally three teenagers from the rear began heading toward them. "We'll go."

"No!" A large man stepped in front of them. "I won't allow it."

"Get out of the way! How many of them died because of us?" The young man challenged the older. "We at least owe them this much." The two young women behind him locked hands.

The three of them stopped a foot in front of Grace. "We'll go. And we will come back and tell them what we saw."

"Do you have any weapons?" Theron asked.

The redhead to the left dug in her bag and pulled out a pocket knife, holding it up to him. "This is it. You can have it."

He smiled down at her. "You can keep it."

The other two shook their heads, indicating they were free of weapons.

The brunette girl looked at Nala. "So, you're like a werewolf, huh?"

"Yes." She eyed the girl, but tried to remain calm.

"So do you go all crazy when the moon is full?"

Nala couldn't help, even with the tragedy, the girl's question made her laugh.

The girl's mouth fell slack. "You do?"

"Not in the way you think. But in a way that makes my mate—er, husband happy."

The girls both giggled.

As they crested the hill, the devastation below came into view. The redhead released her girlfriend's hand and covered her mouth. "Oh, my God!" Real tears streamed down her face. "It *was* a wedding."

Grace looked at them over her shoulder. "Four of my people are dead. All of the attackers are also dead. The Pixies, Fae, Dwarves, and Gnomes are still getting their numbers together. The man who officiated the wedding was cut in half."

The brunette dropped to her knees and vomited. As she choked and spit, she cried. "Oh God, please forgive me!"

"Get up!" Theron barked.

Nala shot him a look that told him to shut up, or she'd make him. She knelt next to the girl and put her hand on her back. "I know this is hard, but you need to stand up. We'll get you some water." *Colin, bring me a bottle of water, please.* A moment later he approached with a bottle of water. His eyes widened at the three humans. One was on her knees throwing up. The other stood with her mouth open and tears streaming down her face and the young man had his hands in his pockets and kicked at the grass, shame painted on his face.

Colin handed her the water. "Here," she said, "rinse your mouth before you drink."

The woman did as instructed, swishing and spitting before sipping at the water. "I can't believe you're being so nice." She wiped her tears on the back of her wrist and stood to her feet.

"Would the three of you look at me, please?" Wendy asked.

The humans turned their attention to her.

"For hundreds of years we've all fought each other. It wasn't until Grace, a Lycan who was raised believing she was a human, came to us. It was then we all began to get along. This school was built to integrate our species...to live peacefully among each other. We don't want to hurt humans any more than we want to continue to hurt each other. I'm not saying we don't have bad eggs, just like humans have theirs. But most of us...we just want to live."

The girls locked hands again.

The boy began to sob. "We understand."

"Very well. Now, we're going to walk past the wounded and into the school. Are you ready?"

When they nodded, the group led the human trio inside the building after the redhead stopped to gag one more time. Once inside, the heavy air of chaos lifted.

"Holy shit! This is a school?" The guy put his hand on his forehead. "It's like a huge castle."

"Let's start off in the dorms and work our way to the classrooms." Grace flagged them to follow her. She froze in her tracks and closed her eyes. She turned to Nala. "Xander is going to be okay, but it's going to take him a long time to heal from the brain damage. He could be in bed for a few weeks. Gustav is going to get our mother so she can sit with him."

She nodded and silently breathed a sigh of relief.

"Who is Xander?" The brunette asked.

"My brother. His head was crushed by a shifter bear." Grace wiped a tear off her cheek then proceeded toward the dorm.

"Oh my God. Her brother was almost killed and she's taking us on a tour?" The brunette whispered to the redhead.

Grace spun on her heel until she was in the brunette's face. "Little girl, he almost died because of you...humans. Yes, I'm giving you a tour and trying to remain calm because you need to see we are just like you. I'm showing you how we live so you can tell the rest of them so this doesn't happen anymore. Do you understand? This is difficult for me. But my hearing is much better than yours, so please keep your comments to yourself until you leave."

"Ma'am," her face pale, she cleared her throat, "what I, uh, meant was, maybe someone else should give us the tour so you can be with your brother. Please. We've obviously done enough harm."

Her shoulders slumped forward. "I'm sorry. You're right." She took a step backward. "Zoltar, if you would do the honors."

"Of course, go." He stood for a moment as Grace shifted and ran off toward the makeshift hospital. Once she was out of sight, he pasted a smile on his face, which shocked Nala.

"So, uh..." The young man shifted his weight, "so you have actual dorms?"

Zoltar put his arm around the man's shoulder. Nala tried not to laugh when the human tensed.

"They're much nicer than you're used to, but come and see for yourself."

The Centaur looked like a mountain compared to the thin human. When he opened the door to a room, the humans rushed in. "Do you take human students?"

Wendy chuckled. "We hadn't thought about it, but as you know, until now, we were just a myth to you."

"Oh man," the redhead blurted, "we could like...pay tuition and stuff. We could be ambassadors."

Nala could feel the supernatural eyes roll in the room. "That's actually not a bad idea, Wendy. How is it any different than Gnome settlements among Lycans? We're all about integration. Maybe if they see human students attending our school and stay human and alive...they could see we're not dangerous."

"But we are dangerous, Nala." Zoltar spoke up. "We could hurt them on accident sparring or just...kids being kids and roughhousing."

"It's not like you're eating us though. Those are accidents." The redhead looked hopeful. "Look the girl that came to us said you guys were like, creatures of the night, all gnashing of teeth and stuff. But this is an actual college right? You're accredited and stuff?"

"Wait? What girl?" Wendy stepped forward and stared the girl in the eye. "Brittany!" She gasped. "Zoltar ran out of the room."

"What just happened?" The brunette looked at Nala.

Wendy grabbed the girl's wrist and stared her in the eye again. "Think about what you know. Why you are here."

The girl stared back at her. "You're like...you're inside my head. Holy fucking shit! You're inside my head!"

After releasing her she stepped back and leaned against a wall to steady herself. "Nala... I'm...Oh shit."

Water gushed out from Wendy's dress.

"Wait, you're not *that* pregnant yet!" She ran to her side. "Sit down."

"Whoa. What's going on?" The human male asked.

"Centaurs don't gestate that long. I think all of this action...Ouch!" She clutched her stomach. "Shit! Contraction! Shit! Grace!" She screamed.

Zoltar and Grace rushed into the dorm room seconds later.

"Ow!" Wendy cried.

"Towels, we need towels." The redhead fanned her

hands in the air.

"Straight behind you," Grace waved. "Light is on the right. Towels are in the cabinet."

The redhead ran and returned in seconds with four towels. "Lay her down."

"Do you know what you're doing?" Zoltar's face burned red.

"Look man, I grew up on a farm. I've delivered four horses and one baby. I don't know what's going to come out of there, but I know what I'm doing. Now hold her hand."

"I don't even know your name," Wendy cried.

"Oh honey, my name is Susan. I'm going to help you deliver your baby, okay, but I need you to do as I tell you to. Your water broke so there's no stopping the birth. When is your due date?" She laid a towel by Wendy's rear and draped another over her own lap.

"We figured three weeks." Zoltar held onto Wendy's hand.

"Okay, and how long is a normal pregnancy?"

"Five months."

The girl looked into the air and started counting. "Okay, at that rate, your baby might be a little small, but can live outside the womb. So what I want you to do is take a deep breath and let it out. Do it three times."

Wendy did as she asked. While she was breathing, the girl looked at Nala. "I need some scissors and a sterile knife. Dental floss would be great too if you can find it…and a bottle of liquor, something high proof."

Grace jumped up. "I'll get it." She scrambled into the kitchen.

When she came back, she had a large bowl with everything in it.

"Okay Wendy, what I'm going to do now is cut off your panties. They're pretty, but they're already ruined. Are you okay with that?"

"Cut them off!" she screamed.

Susan smiled. "Keep breathing. No pushing yet." She lifted up Wendy's skirt. The human male passed out, hitting the floor hard. Ignoring him, she went to work, cutting away the panties and pulling the material, tossing them on the floor.

"Ow, ow, ow!"

"No, don't do that." Susan put her hands on Wendy's knees. "Listen, I want you to say this with me, breathing through the words. Who. Who. He."

"Who, who, he. Who, who, he."

She nodded. "Very good, that's a bit of Lamaze breathing. It'll keep you from pushing too soon." She explained she was going to check Wendy's dilatation. Zoltar, who normally looked like a bronze statue turned an odd shade of grey.

"Don't you pass out on me, or I'll kick your Centaur ass all over this school!" Wendy screamed.

Grace grabbed Wendy's other hand. "Look at me, Wendy. Good. You feel no pain. The only thing you feel is glee that you're about to meet your son or daughter for the first time. Okay? Total elation."

Susan's mouth fell open as Wendy calmed down. "Keep breathing." She looked to Grace, "explain to her just the way you did, she'll feel pressure and when she feels that pressure, she needs to push. Your voice seems to do something."

Grace repeated the instructions.

"It's a royal thing," Nala whispered to her. "It's sort of like they can control some things in another being."

"Sweet!" The brunette knelt down next to Susan. "I'm Fawn. Weird name for a human, I know, but there you have it."

"Go put lukewarm water in the bowl and bring it back."

Fawn grabbed the bowl and headed to the kitchen.

"The pressure. I feel the pressure. I *feel* the *pressure!*" Wendy huffed.

"Good, now push! Hold to ten. One, two, three, four,

five, six, seven, eight. Stop."

Wendy blew out a large breath of air. "What is it?"

"No biggie," Susan said, "the cord is wrapped around the baby's neck. It happens all of the time. I just have to unwrap it before you push. Breath like I said, who, who, he."

Sweat rolled off her face as she breathed the words. Susan made quick work of unwrapping the cord. "Okay, whenever you're ready, push!"

She gave one hard push and the baby came out. It was small, but looked good. Susan dipped the end of one towel into water and started wiping the babies face. It finally let out a cry. "You have a beautiful baby girl." She placed the girl on Wendy's chest. Tying the floss around the cord, it severed the connection. "Um, Mom might want to hand the baby to Dad."

"Why?" Zoltar asked. "Is she okay?"

"Fawn, go get a few more towels. We have another baby crowning."

"What?" Wendy's eyes widened.

Zoltar's mouth fell open. "What?"

"Yeah, I see it crowning. Okay, Wendy, whenever you feel the pressure, go ahead and push."

"I can't. I can't." Wendy cried.

"You can. Ready?" Susan smiled. "You can do it."

Nala could hear her own heartbeat in her ears and it was thundering. A tear trickled down her cheek.

"Ow!" Wendy yelled before she pushed. The baby's head popped out with the blackest hair Nala had ever seen. It looked different though, like the baby was face down. No…that's a rump. The next child was coming out in Centaur form, butt first.

"Take a deep breath and push again!" Susan yelled. The baby came the rest of the way out. The black little horse body shimmered then morphed into human. "A boy!" Her eyes widened. "I think."

After placing the baby on Wendy's chest, she severed the

cord and folded the mess in the towel.

"Twins. Z! We have twins!"

"At least one of them came out half a horse," Susan stood, scooping up the towels. "He came out that way, anyway. I'm sorry. I don't know how it works for you."

"Congratulations!" Grace sniffed.

"Yes, congratulations," Nala cried, "that was beautiful." So much chaos and violence was suddenly overshadowed by the beautiful delivery of two healthy babies. The energy in the room was completely positive and happy. She wiped her eyes on the back of her hands.

Zoltar kissed Wendy's forehead. "Thank you for the greatest gift. I can't believe my eyes. Wait until the herd finds out."

Fawn and Susan went to the kitchen and washed their hands. Nala followed them. "Ladies?"

They turned to her.

"I want to thank you for what you just did. I know it was…different."

Susan slid down the cabinet onto the floor and began sobbing. "Are you kidding?"

Unable to contain the shock on her face, Nala bent down. "Uh, are you okay?"

"We could have killed the mother…and those babies." Her face in her hands she continued sobbing. "Innocent lives."

Fawn patted her shoulder. "We didn't know. That lady said they were like Satan worshipers and sacrificing humans and stuff."

Nala set her jaw, determined to decimate whoever was behind this absurd ploy. "As I said, we're not all bad people. Sure, we have some bad apples, but then again so do you. Right? Just like Wendy said outside."

Susan paused and looked up at Nala. The skin around her eyes began to swell and turn red. "Right."

"Let's make a promise to each other." She stood and held her hand out to Susan, who used it to stand to her feet.

"Okay?"

"Let's both do what we can to decrease the fear. Maybe if we understand each other a bit more, we can coexist. Less casualties means both sides win."

Nala heard a high pitched shriek come from the other room. "Babies!" Mary had apparently been made aware of the births.

Susan, Nala, and Fawn giggled, easing the tension in the air.

"Truly, what you did for Wendy was amazing. You stayed very calm. Both babies came out fine. Not really part of the tour but…thank you."

"It's time for the tour to end. Escort them from the property so we can lock down security." Graced pushed through her mind. Nala shivered and asked the women to follow her.

Fawn collected the human male who stared at the floor like he saw the slightest sign of the birth, he might pass out.

"Congratulations on the babies." Susan gave a weak smile to Wendy and Zoltar who were holding their newborns. She turned to Mary. "I'm very sorry about your wedding day. If there is anything I can ever do for you…" Reaching in her back pocket, she pulled out a card. "This is my phone number. Don't hesitate to ask. I will do whatever I can to earn your forgiveness."

Mary stared at the card she was about to accept and pushed it back at Susan. "You delivered Wendy's babies. That is enough for me. You are forgiven. Just tell the other humans to leave us alone."

Fawn clutched her arm and choked back a sniffle. "Thank you ma'am. We should be going."

Mary turned her attention to the two tiny bundles of joy.

As Nala led the women from the school, her mind raced. How could they stay hidden now? The humans wouldn't keep the secret. Not after Gustav turned three of them. A thought occurred to her. "May I have that business card?"

"Uh, sure." Susan reached in her bag and pulled it out, handing it over.

"Maybe we can grab coffee sometime soon. We can talk. I can answer your questions as I'm sure you have plenty. I know Grace did when she came to us."

The women looked at her, puzzled.

"Sure. That would be lovely." Susan bobbed her head, her eyes wide. "You drink coffee?"

"Don't you?"

Her face reddened. "Ignore me."

Once outside, Nala saw most of the carnage had already been cleaned up. The group of anxious humans rested at the top of the hill, guarded by a very angry Gustav.

"What did you see?" one man asked Fawn as they approached.

Fawn cried out. "We almost killed babies! That's what! *We* are the barbarians here. We need to leave these people alone. We destroyed a wedding and almost killed babies! Babies!" She slapped the man hard in the chest with both hands as she repeated the word "babies."

"What babies?" he asked.

"Agh!" She threw her hands up and stomped to the back of the crowd. "I'm going home. We should all be ashamed of ourselves. Every last one of us!"

"Susan?" The woman clutching the bible approached.

"I just delivered two premature babies that wouldn't have arrived tonight had we not attacked. They're both doing okay, so far as I can tell and no thanks to us." She shook her head. "They were very kind to us. Pete wouldn't know anything. He passed out as soon as the woman went into labor."

The human male she called Pete shrugged his shoulders. "Sorry. But they were nice while I was awake. And the woman whose wedding we destroyed said she forgave us. That's all I know."

There were several mumbles as they walked away. Nala turned to Gustav. "So you have three new children too."

He sighed. "Yes, biting them was one thing. I've never turned anyone out of anger. This...is new." Looking at the three frightened men standing in a group he shook his head. "They're terrified of me."

She wanted to offer words of encouragement, but, "Show them different," was all she could muster. As soon as the words left her mouth, Gustav and his new entourage disappeared.

Colin, I want to go home.

"Not yet, we have to meet with the royals and due to Wendy's birth, we're all meeting in their apartment. It's about to be cramped. Come on back."

Great. She sighed as she trudged back toward the school.

ELEVEN

"Well there's no containing it now!" Beauregard's voice was low, probably due to the new life inside the room, but anger bubbled in his words.

"No," Zoltar stood, holding his daughter. "Containment is over. We need a plan to reach out to their government, to reassure them there is nothing to fear."

Nala cleared her throat to gather attention. "I'm sorry, I know I'm not a royal, but they should be afraid. Not all of our species is like minded. Just as I suggested to the human, we have our bad apples just like they do. And I'm sure there will be attacks, just to draw attention to us." She was exhausted and felt a little nauseous. Battling on an empty stomach didn't seem to be setting well with her.

Grace stood, her face long. "I'm overwhelmed with joy at the birth of Wendy and Zoltar's children. However, two dozen of our students are either dead, or have defected to the Separatists. We've lost some our own tonight and Xander is in really bad shape. We don't have time for bickering or wavering. Beauregard, you are head of FOSE for now. We need a delegation and now. By daylight, I want names. We'll get a few of our human teachers to sit with them and get them ready to meet the humans. I really think television is the way to go. I'll reach out to a news station for an exclusive or something. We'll schedule it so we have time to prepare. However, I strongly suggest that Ella and Theron have places on that list."

"Me?" Ella shrieked. "Why?"

"You've very charming. The humans will eat you up, figuratively speaking of course. Theron, well, he's charming and the cameras will love him. One of each species, including the Gnomes, on the list. They show a more docile side, or at least that's how it'll play on TV. Anyone else have anything to add?"

Colin grabbed Nala's hand and squeezed.

"Yes," Zoltar said. "Brittany Merrill escaped. I was called back because Wendy was in labor and I lost her."

Grace thought for a moment. "Well, at least we have a place to start looking. Goodnight everyone."

Colin and Nala wasted no time getting to the car.

As soon as they cleared the school's long drive, Colin let out a gasp. "Your mind is racing. I can't tell what you're thinking about."

"Everything." It was true. She was thinking about her upcoming fight for Alpha, having a family of her own, dealing with the humans, the fact that she was an aunt, worrying about Richard and Trina, not to mention Xander.

"That explains the frenzy of thoughts and emotions I'm getting from you. How about you pick a topic and we talk."

She looked at him, his eyes filled with worry. He desperately wanted to know what his mate was thinking and feeling. She relented. "You're an uncle."

His lips curved into a smile. "And you're an aunt."

"I want to be a mother," she said quietly. "If I survive this, I'd very much like to discuss starting a family."

"Oh." He turned his head and looked her face on. "Oh!"

"Watch where you're going!" she yelled.

His head snapped forward. "Sorry."

"I'm worried about Xander," she confessed. "His head was crushed by the bear."

"Yeah, that was horrible. He still hasn't shifted on his own to heal. The Fae are working on him and Michelle is with him."

Her heart sank. "I am also worried about Richard and Trina, what Stephany is putting them through."

"They have the choice to come back. It's up to them to accept our whole pack, just as you told them."

Lower Lycans, that's what she'd called them. Memories of cages and shackles flooded her mind.

"And the fight to the death I have in a few short days."

He didn't respond this time and she could only assume it's because the no quarter battle had his nerves on edge as well.

"So, pups, huh? I like the sound of that." Without looking, he reached over and scooped her hand in his. "As long as they have my taste in clothes."

A small laugh gave her the tension relief she needed, as did the warmth of her mate's hand cradling her own.

"I'm going to have coffee with the girl that delivered Wendy's babies." She blurted it out for fear if she didn't, she would fail to tell him.

His brows rose toward his hair line. "Really? Why?"

"I'm going to invite her to the battle."

"What? Are you nuts?"

"Colin, if we willingly show her the worst, then…I don't know. It seems like a good idea. Let her see a woman in power, fighting, literally to keep it. I'd like her to see the pack, how we are." Taking a deep breath, she released it. "The time for secrets is over. There will be humans poking around now, like it or not. I'd rather it be at our invitation. At least that way I have some control over the situation."

After what seemed like a lifetime of silence, his chin lifted and fell. "You know what? That's not a bad idea. We have to inform the pack tonight anyway."

She looked down at her shredded blood stained dress.

"You know, if I keep coming home this way, they may never let me leave again."

"I may never let you leave again…or dress up. This is getting ridiculous."

When he pulled into the parking spot, she could see the entire pack already gathered by the fire. "No need to call a meeting then."

Eyes widened as they approached, both of them showing signs of a battle. Colin, who usually looked very put together had no tux jacket, his shirt was untucked and his tie missing. Nala's torn and bloody dress set the tone.

"What the fuck, man?" Jake ran over. "Are you two okay?"

"I have an announcement," Nala called over the crowd. "A large group of humans was made aware of our presence this evening. Suffice it to say, we've been made. Also of note, Zoltar, the Centaur King, and Wendy, our pack, er— the Centaur Queen have had twins this evening. Both seem to be doing well. They had one boy and one girl."

The crowd erupted into cheers but only briefly.

"Now I know the thought of humans' knowledge of us might be unsettling and we are heading into uncharted water. Therefore, I'm taking the bold step of inviting one woman here to our land and to the no quarter battle with Mr. Kincade. She is to be treated as my guest. Anyone mistreating her will be sanctioned—heavily. Now, I need a shower, so I bid you a good night."

She turned from her pack. "Wait!"

Kendra, one of her youngest pack mates from Scottsboro stepped to the front of the crowd. "How did the humans find out about us?"

Nala stared at the young girl, her red hair knotted in an intricate braid, green eyes wide as she waited for an answer.

"The Separatists, we think. It was an inside job, someone at the school." Suddenly, she realized she'd dumped scary information on them with little hope or guidance. "The royals have a plan to come out on national television to show that we're not barbarians. For now, our rules still apply. No shifting in front of humans, with the exception of the one I'll have here. Stay in human form while in town. No fighting with them and avoid conflict when you can." She searched her mind for the right words.

"We're very exhausted; as I'm sure you can understand." Colin spoke up. "Nala suggested to me in the car that we have a morning meeting tomorrow after breakfast to clear up any questions. We'll meet in the hall then. It'll give us all time to think."

She was relieved to have him come to her aid. Over his shoulder, she saw the rump of a centaur. "What the hell?"

Jake stepped in her line of sight. "Extra security. We had trespassers while you were at the party. Prometheus insisted you get your rest before the fight. There will be no ambush on his watch. I approved it, acting in your absence. So just go take your shower. Get some sleep and accept that this is for the good of the pack."

She wanted to protest. Lycans didn't need Centaur security. But she was too tired for a fight so she slapped him on his shoulder. "Good work."

Colin's arm slid around her as she made her way into the house.

"Hey."

His tired smile met hers. "Hey."

"Thanks for stepping in. My brain is just...I think it's melting." Each stair seemed like it was taller than the next as she climbed to the second level. Never in her life had she remembered feeling so exhausted.

When they reached their room, she headed straight for the bathroom, stripping and stepping into the hot shower. While the thought of lingering in the hot water tempted her, exhaustion won over and she made quick work of getting clean and stepping out.

Wrapped in a towel, she stepped out of the bathroom and found Colin sitting at the edge of the bed. "I'll be out in five or less. Try not to pass out on me."

After shedding the towel, she climbed under the sheets and stared at the ceiling. Her heat had never come. Seeing the twin babies made her ache for a family of her own, but what responsible mother would sit as Alpha? Who could balance the position of Alpha with the demands of motherhood? It mattered not as it seemed Jagger's damage may last her a lifetime. She'd taken strong measures to ensure she didn't sire his children and for that, she may never have any of her own.

Colin deserved a family. He'd been robbed of one already.

"Stop!" he said from the bathroom door. Water ran from his hair down his naked body as he hadn't bothered drying off. "You're killing yourself in there. We don't know anything about your heat. Just because it didn't come yet, doesn't mean it never will. We'll have Dr. Maryann check on you when you're ready. But fuck, Nala! What's the difference between an Alpha mother and an Alpha father?" He snatched his towel off the rack and dried his hair as he made his way toward the bed.

"I'm sorry. What?"

"You wondered what kind of mother you would be. You'd be the same strong leader as any Alpha with a family. You shouldn't accept challenges while pregnant, but that's not a big deal. Many Alpha's have let their Beta fight on their behalf. That's the way it has been since the beginning. You may be a woman, but you're under the same rules as the rest. You don't have an extra burden because you're a woman."

She sat speechless as she watched him dry off. His tone oozed lecture, but his words were...empowering.

"Colin, I...I forget we're connected. I'm sorry."

"You forget because I close you out. I'm going to stop doing that. I'm going to let all of my fears and concerns flood in for you so you can see. You can feel me here for you."

Her heart raced. The overwhelming fatigue had fled as her gaze traveled the beautiful form of her mate. He was strong, toned, and his skin had a sun kissed glow.

"Have I told you, how much I love you?" Her lips tightened in a smirk. "How wonderful it is to have a mate who isn't intimated by me?" She sucked in her bottom lip as he crawled onto the bed.

"Intimidated? Not at all. Worried, sometimes. Frustrated—always!" His fingers wrapped around the top of the sheet and he flipped it back, exposing her naked body. "I have to fight the urge to keep you in this bed twenty-four seven."

She giggled as he dove in toward her neck, playfully biting at her collar bone. "I think you need a distraction," he said before nipping at her ear lobe.

"Oh yes, distract me. Please," she gasped out.

The walls he had up came crashing down and she could feel his raw emotions. He was in awe of her, of her strength, and frustrated by her concerns. More than anything, he was completely smitten with her. If his thoughts and emotions didn't tell her, the firmness of his erect shaft certainly did.

His lips trailed down her collar bone to her right breast, as he kissed his way around the circumference before gently licking at her erect nipple. Gooseflesh formed where his lips met her skin. A drop of cold water fell from his wet hair onto her stomach, causing her to flinch.

His gaze met hers as a devilish grin spread across his lips. Ducking his head, he edged back until his lips landed between her legs. Parting her with this tongue, he caressed her bud, which was quick to harden under his attention. Warmth pooled low in her belly and she fisted his damp hair, pulling his mouth harder against her pussy.

He hummed while teasing her clit with his tongue, sending tingles of pleasure to her core. She bucked her hips, grinding into his mouth. She released his hair to clutch the sheets, giving her what little leverage they had to offer.

His hands ran up her thighs then he tucked them under her ass, squeezing the cheeks, and holding her firmly in place as he brought her to her crest. A pleasurable ache crept from her belly to her breasts, making them full and heavy. She cupped them as she cried out in orgasm.

After a few light kisses to her inner thigh, he scooted up next to her, gently rolling her to the side. He grazed her entrance with the head of his cock, gathering her juices on the tip before gliding in, rocketing her orgasm once again.

His deep guttural moan had an effect on her. She pushed back against his cock, sending it deeper inside her, releasing a gasp of her own. Her mate, filled her inside. His hand slid down the length of her torso, over her hip and pulled a thigh over his hip, then trailed back up, massaging her sensitive, orgasm wracked clit as he thrust and retreated, again and again.

Orgasmic tremors rocked her as he fucked and teased her. Turning her head far as she could, she screamed into a pillow as his final thrust released his seed into her.

"Colin!" she gasped.

"You feel so damned good," he said through labored breaths.

She laughed while fighting for air. "So do you. That was intense."

After covering them both with the sheets, he spooned into her, kissing her neck. "Nala, my love, you are my family. If pups come along, then so be it. But you should know I'm quite content with you. No, not content. I'm elated to have you as my mate."

Her eyes stung at his words. She blinked to fight back the tears. "Thank you."

"Thank you," he whispered.

TWELVE

The meeting the following morning was as expected. Most of the Lycans were frightened at the thought of human awareness. Nala, Colin, and Jake did the best they could to field questions from the pack. When Nala reminded them that some of them had faced intolerable cruelty from their own kind, it seemed to bring things back around.

"As I said, I intend to invite a human here today so you can meet her, to see that like us, they're not all alike." Not a word was spoken after that, and the meeting was adjourned. Her call to Susan went well, and she'd agreed to meet for coffee.

Nala went alone, much to the chagrin of her mate and her Beta. She arrived early and scanned the area. Nothing seemed out of sorts. Comfortable that she was safe, she ordered her beverage and took a seat in the corner. Susan arrived a few moments later.

The two women stared at each other for a brief moment, neither seeming to know how to start the conversation.

"I think it's important, to start a dialog," Nala began.

Susan let out a large breath. "Thank you for starting. I didn't know what to say."

She clutched her mug. "I have a crazy idea and I'm not sure you're up for it. So I am relying on you to tell me if any of it makes you uncomfortable." Silently, she prayed to the gods that her plan would work.

"Crazy ideas invented the light bulb, electricity, the internet, and Cheetohs. Lay it on me." Susan leaned in on her elbows and sipped at her coffee.

Nala pulled her shoulders back, sitting a little higher. "Our introduction was under...unusual circumstances, but we've been introduced nonetheless. We can't change how that happened. However, I think to give you an accurate depiction, I need to show you the best of us *and* the worst."

The color left Susan's face. "The worst?"

Nala quickly filled Susan in on her past, how she came to be the Alpha and that female Alphas were unheard of. "I'd like to show you how we live. Then, you will be present for my no quarter challenge. It will be gruesome and someone will die. Can you cope with that?"

Her mouth hung open as she stared at Nala. "No quarter...that means..."

"No mercy, fight to the death." She stared into the woman's eyes, trying to gauge her reaction. "There will be blood. But you seem to be able to handle that."

"Blood from birth is one thing. It's life. It's the creation of life. But..." She stopped, shaking her head and squeezing her eyes shut. "Never mind, I have an open mind. Who am I to be squeamish if it's your life on the line?"

Content with her answer, Nala stood from the table. "I'm in the Honda Accord. You can follow me."

"No!" Susan stood from her chair and slung her bag over her shoulder. I'm riding with you. You have the responsibility to drive me home. Got it? I took the bus here anyway. But, still. This way you have to win. You have no choice because you have to fulfill your responsibility to me."

Crazy human! "That's not really the way it works, but I

take the responsibility anyway."

Susan followed her to her car. The drive back to pack property was filled with questions from Susan. "So, this is the beginning of women's rights for you then, huh?"

"Yes, as I said, Grace was raised thinking she was a human. So when she came to us, she was appalled at the lack of, well, position for the females. She took very drastic measures. My Alpha had kidnapped her because of her royal blood. The rest, we already covered."

She shook her head. "That's some real medieval shit."

Nala laughed. "We're working on it."

"So, interspecies breeding is a new thing then?"

This topic was a bit more uncomfortable for her. "Well, it was rare before, as far as I know. But, yes, we are beginning to live and, uh, love together."

"I can see why. Shifter men are fuckin' hot!"

A violent burst of laughter erupted from Nala. It must've startled Susan because she jumped.

"I'm sorry. But yes, I can see our men are of better stock. They don't faint at the sight of birth."

"Hey, your Centaur turned all grey. I thought we would lose him too!" She smiled and put her palm on her forehead. "Oh God, don't judge us all on the account of Pete. He's always been a bit of a panty waste." She rubbed her forehead before putting her hand back in her lap.

"Human men can't all be that bad. Can they?" Nala glanced at her as she turned onto the drive to the pack property.

"Good ones are hard to find."

"Well, I can tell you shifter men are excellent lovers if you're ever interested. By the way, welcome to the Belfast pack's property."

She leaned forward in her seat, taking in the view. "Holy shit. Look at this place! It's breathtaking." Her head shot from left to right and back. "Look at all the houses. You are all hidden very well."

Nala hoped her people behaved and received Susan well.

She put the car in park and turned off the engine. "Home sweet home."

A small group of Gnomes had gathered as they exited the car. Thomas approached with a small box. "We made this for our honored guest."

Susan put her hand over her mouth. "Wow. Really?" She took the box from Thomas and slowly opened it. Inside, Nala could see a set of beautiful handmade garnet earrings. "You *made* these?"

Molly, a tiny Gnome with a jet black bun affixed to the top of her head nodded. "I made the earrings. Thomas carved the stones and set them."

"That's very generous. Thank you so very much." She looked at Nala. "This is too much."

Shaking her head, she winked down at her friends. "It's best not to argue with a gift from the Gnomes. They're very sweet that way."

Molly skipped over to Nala. "I think she likes them."

"I thank you for making them. That was very kind."

Four pups came bounding toward them.

"Puppies!" She began to crouch down and pet them. "Oh God! These are your people's children. Not puppies. What...what can I do? Is it okay to touch them?"

With a smile and a nod she urged on. "You can treat them as you would any other puppies. They love the attention. And yes, we call our children pups. It's okay. Scratch their tummies. Pat their bottoms. They love it." She knelt next to Susan, realizing how foreign it was to the human. The pups jumped, rolled around and kissed Susan's face.

"They're so sweet."

"Okay kids. Let's let her past the driveway. Off you go." Several whines were heard as they pups began walking away.

Nala gave her a tour of their land, ending with the pack house where their guest joined them for dinner.

"Whoa, whoa...human's don't eat this much," she protested. Her eyes bulged as she looked down at the plate piled high with food.

"Lycans have a high metabolism. We have to eat a lot to keep up our strength." Colin had joined them, much to Nala's relief. "Just scoot whatever you don't want on Jake's plate. He eats as much as three of us."

Jake lifted his plate toward her. "That's right. I'll take it all!"

Her face burned red. A sheepish grin spread across her lips as she shifted three quarters of her contents onto his plate. "So," she began, "it's like this all of the time. Big meals together like one big happy family?"

Nala forced a smile as she looked down at her plate. Her fight was in a few hours. The thought of which made her nauseous. "Yes, unless these two are nipping at each other's hind quarters." She waved between Colin and Jake.

Jake smiled as she tore off a hunk of bread. "It's a sibling thing. Do you humans have that? Sibling rivalry?"

With a snicker, Susan waved her fork in the air and swirled it around. "I shaved a bald spot on my sister's head one night while she was sleeping."

Several around the table joined her laughter. "So that's a yes, then?" Jake winked.

He's flirting with the human?

"My brother would flirt with a tree if it were receptive." Colin rolled his eyes.

Nala's wolf stirred and whined. Colin must've noticed because his smiled turned into a hardened stare. He nodded. *"Easy girl. You'll do fine during the fight. None of us will let them pull anything. We've a plan in place if they fight dirty."*

Protect your mate. Protect her at all costs. For the pack. For the family. Her silent wolf uttered words for the first time in weeks.

Nala felt Colin's wolf stir.

Jake stopped chewing and scooted from the table. "Excuse me."

Everyone at the table fell silent.

Susan looked around. "Was it something I said?"

Colin placed his fork on the table and scooted his plate away. "Did Nala explain our wolves reside in our head when we're in human form…that they have thoughts and feelings too?"

Her head shook.

"Her wolf is…restless because of the fight. Mine picked up on it because we're mated. Jake, being her Beta, or second in command, is also on edge. We're just picking up on pre-fight jitters. I'm sorry if it's uncomfortable."

Nala swallowed the lump in her throat. Food was certainly out of the question. "Do you remember how I said I wanted you to see the best and the worst of us?"

Susan nodded.

Nala searched for the words. "I don't want to color your opinion of others. However, all I have to offer is my own knowledge. The pack that's coming tonight, they originated from Chicago. They're very greedy and power hungry. They outgrew Chicago and had to expand. Most Lycans are content staying in their packs, on pack land. Most don't ever expand. Expansion is unheard of, for the most part. Anyway, they're looking to take our land, push us out or claim us as their slaves or something."

"Slaves! No!" She crossed her arms over her chest. "It's the twenty-first century. We don't do slaves anymore!"

Nala couldn't help but smile at the woman. "I'm not sure what she means exactly when she says, 'Lower Lycan,' but it can't be good."

"Lower Lycan? I don't like this bitch already and I just found out about Lycans." She tossed her napkin on her plate. "Why don't you just blow them away?"

"What, like you guys did at the school?" Tracy's glare bore through her.

"Tracy!" Nala growled. Her eyes glowed.

Susan's mouth fell open. She regained her composure quickly. "No, I had that coming. Cool eyes by the way. Now I'm totally jealous." She turned to Tracy. "We were ignorant. There's no denying that. So. Touché."

"It's just not the way we handle things. Hand to hand combat, to show who the bigger man, or in my case, woman, is." Nala shot another look at her closest confidant.

"Apologies." Tracy stood up and started gathering plates. "It's just...what's to keep your kind from doing that to us again? And what do we do? Get guns of our own?"

"Yes." The voice was quiet and solemn as it slipped out of Susan's mouth.

"Humans have guns. You might want to get a few of your own. You know...for protection."

The look of shock on Tracy's face was shared by many around the table.

"We're not going to start killing humans. Diplomacy is the plan. The royals can handle this." Nala's tone spoke that it was the end of the discussion...for now at least.

Jake trotted back into the dining area, sweat glistening on his forehead. "Sorry if I was rude."

Unable to decipher what was going on with her Beta, Nala chose to ignore him. "Jake, I need to prepare for the fight tonight. Would you please take care of our guest until then?"

"It would be a pleasure."

He smiled at Susan.

She blushed.

Nala and Colin shot each other a glance. *Flirting,* they both thought simultaneously.

Thirteen

The sun had set. Nala stood on the deck with Colin, peering out at the land. Neither of them spoke, the silence between them saying enough. Colin knew the pressure his mate was under and that tiny piece of knowledge was the comfort she needed.

In the distance, she could hear the crunching of gravel under rubber tires. They were approaching…in vehicles. That was very unusual for their kind, but the Scottsboro pack was one of showmanship. The Belfast pack gathered ranks, circling around, facing the newcomers. Susan stood next to Jake, which made Nala feel a bit more comfortable. Scottsboro Lycans would sniff her out immediately. The pack and the Beta were there to protect her if they had any funny ideas.

"A human at a no quarter battle. That's funny Baker." Stephany rolled her eyes. "Is this the new rage, mingling with humans?"

"It's part of our integration plan, yes." Nala pushed through the Belfast crowd to the front.

Wearing knee length leather boots, leggings and a dress

that barely covered her ass, Stephany Kincade smirked back at Nala. "Ready to die, were-bitch?"

"Not today. Thanks. Where's my challenger? Bad hair day?"

Jackson Kincade stepped out of a canary yellow Humvee and shirked off a leather jacket. He looked ready for war, wearing camo pants, a black muscle shirt and combat boots.

"Cute outfit." Nala winked at him.

He growled in return.

Her stomach lurched again, but she forced herself to smile through it.

Richard and Trina edged their way to the front.

Nala's gaze immediately fell on them. Trina looked like she'd lost weight. Her eyes were sunken in and her hair looked filthy. "Ready to come home yet?" *Please say yes. Please.*

Trina opened her mouth to speak but before anything could come out of her mouth, Richard's arm flew around her shoulders. "We're fine, thanks."

She only stared at Trina, hoping the woman would come to her senses.

Jake stepped to the front of the crowd. "This way, please." He led them to a clear field of grass.

Susan was surrounded, shoulder to shoulder, by Belfast pack members during the walk. When they reached the clearing, a circle formed for the fight, Belfast on one side, Scottsboro on the other.

Jake stepped to the center. "Rules have been the same for centuries. This is a no quarter battle between Nala Baker, Alpha of the Belfast pack, and Jackson Kincade, challenger. No one is to interfere under penalty of death. The only person who can stop the fight is one of the opponents. You may fight in either human or Lycan form. Any questions?"

After a moment of silence, Susan stepped forward. "I have a question."

"Figures," Stephany spat.

"You're fighting for this land. Right? For the right to rule it?" She glared at Stephany.

"Yes, yes, and if you weren't a stupid human, you'd know this."

She smirked back at Stephany Kincade with disgust. "Then if she wins, does she win your land? Seems only fair."

Colin spoke up. "That's not how it works. If Nala wins—s"

"She won't," Stephany huffed.

"If she wins, she gets to keep her land and her life. The loser will have lost their life so it's square."

Susan stepped back in the crowd, keeping her eyes on Stephany.

I don't trust her either. Smart human.

"Let the battle begin." Jake stepped back, edging through the crowd until he was next to Susan.

Nala squared off, standing still as she watched Jackson bounce on his feet like a pro-boxer. She stood still, weight on the balls of her feet, ready to move.

Deep breath in. Good. Deep breath out. Fake to the left, fake to the right. What is he doing? Jackson bounced around, air boxing to himself. Nala shook her head. "Are we fighting, or do you have an imaginary friend over there?"

He lunged at her. She stepped out of the way and he stumbled. *It can't be this easy.*

After righting himself, he resumed bouncing up and down with his fists up in front of his face. She didn't see the jab when it connected with her chin. A flash of white, followed by the sting of pain through her jaw startled her. She took a few steps back and shook her head. It hurt, but it wasn't *horrid.* She loosened her knees and crouched.

When Jackson rushed her again, she lunged slightly, hitting her shoulder into his gut and flipping him over her back. He hit the grass with a hard thud, rolled over to his stomach and pushed off the ground. She backed away a few feet to give herself some room to react.

The pounding of hooves could be heard approaching. She wanted to look, but didn't want to take her eyes off of her opponent. When he looked away, she snuck a glance. Grace and Roman were approaching with the entire herd of Centaurs, including the new parents.

"Wendy, you should be resting," she called over her shoulder.

"Oh I'm rested. Tiff is watching the babies. Zoltar and I wouldn't miss your fight. We're here to be certain it's a fair fight. We have intel they plan an ambush tonight and the royals won't stand for it." She scraped her hoof on the ground.

"You have no right to interfere!" Stephany screeched.

Zoltar laughed. "We're not interfering. We're spectating."

Nala waited until Jackson turned back to her. She wasn't going to take a cheap shot. She kept her eyes on him as he looked to his pack for answers.

"Fight's over here, Jackson."

He turned to face her. The bouncing ceased as he sized her up. A larger crowd seemed to have quelled his antics. The air around him shimmered as he shifted to wolf. Nala followed suit. Jackson crouched and circled. She matched his movement, keeping him at her front where she could defend.

Finally, he leaped at her. She held her ground, waiting until he nearly reached her when she opened her muzzle and clamped onto his leg, pulling hard as she rolled. His side hit the ground with a giant *thud*. When he scrambled to get to his feet, she lurched on top of him and bit down on his shoulder. His warm, salty metallic blood filled her mouth as she bit him once, twice, then three times before jumping to the side.

He righted himself, limping as he edged toward her again.

"Kill her!" Stephany screeched.

Following his mates scream, he lunged at Nala. Both wolves bit and tumbled, rolling on the grass as they took hunks out of each other. White heat seared her face as he tore at the flesh by her jaw.

"Remember your training!" Prometheus's voice boomed through the air.

Nala shifted to human, healing her face. She grabbed a large rock and slung it at Jackson, hitting him in the eye. He yelped and shifted back to human. "Bitch! That's not fair!"

"You're twice my size. Let's talk about fair," she spat the blood that still lingered in her mouth.

He swung at her, his fist connecting with her brow bone. The second she heard the crack of bone, she shifted to wolf, praying the magic would heal her. It did enough to keep her eye from closing, though she could feel her fur wet with blood. She shifted back to human immediately, hiking her leg up, and then crashing her boot down on the side of his knee, buckling it from under him. He fell to his knees and yelled out in pain.

"Watch your back! Their pack is stirring!" Colin's voice called out in her head. She glanced around. They were moving. Something was up. The air glistened as the entire Scottsboro pack shifted, except for Trina who stood glaring at Nala.

Nala's hair stood on end, but she kept her opponent in her sights. That's when she heard it, the thumps of large wolf pads hitting dirt. Another Lycan was approaching. She shifted to wolf and leaped over the top of him, shifting into human, pulling the knife out of her boot and slicing the throat of the beast before landing on her feet.

Stephany screamed. "No weapons!"

"No weapons with my opponent. That was someone interfering. The rules are clear."

Nala could hear Susan's protests over the crowd. "That's not fair. That's cheating. Cheaters!"

"Quiet," Jake urged her. "Pay attention."

A commotion to the left stole her attention. Three of the Scottsboro pack members had grabbed three Gnomes by the throats. Nala froze. Her duty as Alpha was to protect her pack.

"Conceded and they go free," Stephany sneered. Before

Nala could think, the rest of the Gnomes jumped on the three wolves and began clawing and stabbing the wolves with Gnomes in their mouths. Extreme pressure closed around Nala's throat. Her vision blurred. But what happened? She shifted her gaze down to find Jackson Kincade's arm wrapped around her neck, squeezing.

She knew she had mere seconds before she was dead. He wouldn't stop with her blacking out. He called a no quarter battle for a reason.

"Fight. Please fight Nala. This is a piece of shit, punk. You took down Jagger Merrill. Jackson Kincade can't be the end of you. Fight for me. Fight for the pack!" She could hear the tears in Colin's mental voice. He was pleading with her to fight.

Her feet were not touching the ground. Her hands could not reach the man behind her. Her legs kicked but did little damage. *Remember your training.* Blackness began closing around her and her muscles started to twitch. She had to shift but…peace. Peace was creeping in. It was light and airy. No pain. No guilt. No nightmares. Pure, unadulterated peace and tranquility.

"Nala, I love you. Now please, fight for me. Come back to me." Colin! He needed her. He didn't deserve to suffer because of one weak moment. She closed her eyes and focused hard. Her skin blazing as she fought to shift with what tiny energy she had left. Her vision blurred one final time before she felt the tingling over her body as hands and feet were replaced with paws, her face replaced with a muzzle. She scrambled and wriggled until Jackson could no longer hold her neck. He dropped her.

Nala spun, biting his inner thigh where she thought a major artery resided. She chomped down hard, feeling his blood pulse in her mouth. When he fell to the ground she leaped up, locking her jaws around his throat and bit down hard, pulling back until Jackson's lifeless body stopped moving.

"No!" Stephany Kincade dropped to her knees and screamed.

Nala fell back on the ground and stared at the body of Jackson Kincade. Eyes glazed over, throat now a gaping bloody hole. Color already draining from his face, he was gone.

Kill or be killed.

She sat down on her rump and hung her head, crying out. This didn't have to be. No one had to die today. The archaic rules had to be abolished.

"Shh, it's okay." Colin whispered in her ear as he stroked her fur. "You did what you had to do. It's okay."

She leaned her head into his chest and whined.

"Nala, I need you to shift. Your shoulder is dislocated." He held her furry face in his palms. "Please shift."

She hung her head again, after pulling it free from his hands and collapsed on the ground, tears rolling down her furry muzzle. Something was wrong, Colin was right. The pain started to roll up her shoulder, into her neck. She howled out as she shifted.

"We'll clean out the riff raff," Prometheus announced. "Get her to your doctor."

Wendy and Grace rushed to her side. "Wait," Grace said. She sniffed Nala. "Nala! What the hell?"

"What?" She asked as she wiped the tears from her face.

"Wait." Colin closed his eyes then opened them again, wide. "What?"

"What do you mean, what? What the hell are you doing accepting a battle while you're pregnant?" Grace put her hands on her hips. "Oh. Oh! You didn't know?"

"No! I didn't." Tears rolled down her cheeks as she looked at her mate. "I'm sorry, I didn't."

Colin's face burned red. Finally, moisture pooled at his lids. "Pregnant. We're pregnant!"

"You're going to pay for this, bitch!" Stephany screamed as she dragged Jackson's body away. "I'll kill you for this!"

Wendy darted toward her. "I should kill you now!"

"No!" Nala stood with Colin's help. "No more. No more killing. No more death. Let her take her mate home and mourn."

Wendy spun on her heel, her mouth slack. "What?"

"Please, let her go. Let her mourn the loss of her mate. She's upset, as we would all be." She turned to Colin. "Get me to the doctor. I want to make sure this baby is okay."

Wendy's mouth came together as her shock turned into a smile. "I can actually recommend a really good human midwife."

When Nala turned to see what Wendy was looking at, she saw Susan staring at her, tears streaming down her cheeks. "Nala."

Colin helped her to her feet. "I'm sorry. I can only imagine how horrible that was to watch."

"No," she sniffed, "I'm crying because...because I thought you'd lost. I just met you and you're so sweet and...I'm glad you won."

"Baby! I'm going to be a dad! You're going to be the best mom!" Colin's voice was screeching through her head.

"I, uh," she wiped her palms on her pants, "I promised to get you home."

"I'll do it!" Jake jumped in front of Susan. "You go get checked out. I'll take her home, no sweat."

She smiled at him. "Thanks Jake."

Pregnant. Fatigue. Nauseous. Why didn't she see it?

FOURTEEN

Nala lay in bed, stroking her swollen belly. She still had two months to go but the bump in her womb reminded her daily that it was worth the wait.

"Hungry?" Colin kissed her shoulder.

"Can you believe it?"

He ran his palm over her naked belly. The baby kicked where the warmth of his touch met her skin. "He's making sure I do!"

"Or she."

"Or she," he relented with a smile.

"We need to settle on a name," she said with a raised brow.

He scooted up on the bed, sitting Indian style and stared at her stomach. "Okay, lay it on me."

"If it's a girl," she said while running her hand over her baby bump, "I want to name her Gracie May." Because of Grace, she defeated Jagger. Because of Grace, they were moving toward a time of peace. She owed everything to Grace and naming her daughter after such a strong and beautiful Lycan was just the homage she desired.

"If it's a boy?"

"Benjamin. It's a good, strong name." She smiled up at him. "Benjamin Colin Baker."

His head bobbed up and down as he stared at the little foot trying to push through Nala's belly. "I can get behind that."

A knock at the door caused Nala to push her shirt over her belly. "Come in."

Jake's head popped in around the door. "I, uh, need to see you in the conference room."

Nala rolled off the bed and slid her feet into flip flops. "Okay, we're coming." She leaned back, stretching before waddling off after Jake, Colin on her heel.

When they reached the conference room, Tracy and Tom were there waiting.

"What's up?" she asked as she quickly took a seat, edging her belly under the table.

"Tracy has a confession to make," Tom urged. His jaw clenched as he glared at her. "Go on."

She looked down at the table, her eyes swollen from crying. "I did something horrible, but I had the best of intentions."

"Really?" Tom's fist hit the table. "Those were your *best* intentions?"

"Someone had better speak now, before I have to pee, which is like every five minutes." Nala looked at her friend, who appeared as if she'd been up all night crying.

"I'm sorry, Nala. I left those horrible notes for you."

"Notes?" So much had happened she'd forgotten about the threatening notes.

"You looked so bored with things and I knew a little bit of a threat would keep you on your toes. So I left you those nasty notes about being Alpha…like they were some warning." She sobbed into her hands, her fiery red hair spilling over her face.

Nala folded her hands on the table and took a deep breath. "Look at me, please."

Her head tilted up, revealing her green eyes which were bloodshot from crying.

"Did you have any intention of physically hurting me?" She clenched her jaw as she waited for her answer.

Tracy's mouth fell slack. "No! I couldn't. I've loved you like a sister for as long as I could remember."

"So, you betrayed my trust, but to keep me on my toes. Is that right?"

"It sounds horrible. I am horrible."

"As your Alpha, I command you to stop bawling like a pup." She rolled her eyes, irritated at her friend's sobs. It wasn't like Tracy to be a puddle of tears.

She pulled her red hair out of her face and wiped the remainder of her tears on the backs of her hands. "Yes, ma'am."

Nala looked at Tom. "This is enough. The truth is out. Let her go on with her day." She shifted her gaze back to Tracy. "You are forgiven. Don't play games with me again. That's not the relationship we have. Got it?"

She chewed her lip and gave an affirmative nod. "I promise."

The door to the conference room crashed open as Jake ran through it.

"We're in the middle—"

"Shut up," Jake yelled at Tom. He grabbed the remote off the table and turned the television on. "You have to see this!"

Susan was on television, sitting in a faux white leather chair. Video feed of Nala played in the upper left corner of the screen. It was their meeting at the coffee house prior to the battle against Jackson Kincade.

"*So you were invited to their compound?*" The older gentleman interviewing her had dark hair that greyed around his temples. His jaw was set as the tone of his interview grew serious.

"*It wasn't a compound. They live communally, that's true, but it's more like a happy family. Don't paint them out to be the Branch*

Davidians. They were sweet to me. Nala, the woman you see on your screen, she invited me since I was one of the first humans to discover their race. She invited me to see how they lived, who they were."

The man leaned in toward her and adjusted his glasses. *"So you went to them...alone."*

"Yep, and I'm alive and well, sitting here answering your questions." Susan sounded angry, but she kept her face pleasant. Nala felt a smirk come across her face as pride in her new friend washed over her. Poker face wasn't an easy skill to learn.

"This battle. It's very bloody. In fact, she murders that man...right there. She just kills him. Don't you think she should be arrested for that?"

Nala watched the scene play out on the screen, her final killing blow to Jackson. Blood pouring out of his body. Stephany screaming.

"It's the way it's been done for centuries. She's the first female leader in a long time. He came to her property to fight to the death. It was a mutual arrangement, one which she truly wanted to avoid. They just want to live peacefully. In fact, I brought some of my new friends with me today." Mary, Ella, Beauregard, and Theron walked on stage. The silence was deafening.

Mary was the only creature that one could tell was unusual at first. The rest looked like models as they strolled out on stage. The announcer called for a handheld microphone and chairs to be added to the stage.

The TV cut to commercial.

"Holy shit, it's happening." Colin scrubbed his forehead with his hands.

Nala reached over and squeezed his hand. "I'm sure they've thought this through. Just watch."

"Susan is doing a great job. Don't you think?" Jake smiled back at Nala. She could tell he was smitten with her from Jump Street. She could only hope a human-lycan mating would work for him.

The show came back on with everyone sitting in a semi-circle. *"Jeff Jefferson coming to you live from Studio 64. I'm here with* some very interesting guests that have a message."

Ella smiled into the camera. Her flawless features and delicate skin beaming into the camera. *"We have been here the whole time, throughout the centuries, living among you humans. We, as a race of supernatural beings, have no desire to run around and start hurting you. We're working toward a meaningful co-existence with each other, and with you, the humans of the planet. But we, like you, have bad people too. Beauregard here is going to talk to you about that now."*

The camera turned and angled up toward his massive frame. His large arms were crossed over his chest. *"We have developed our own form of government and our own policing agency headed by FOSE, or the Federation of Supernatural Entities. There is a group out there that call themselves Separatists. They are violent and virile. We are currently tracking them down. However, should any human have any threats against them from any non-human, please call the number on your screen. We will deal with them in a swift manner. While I'm on the subject, we've come to you peacefully. We are leaving contact information with this station for the Federal Government here in the United States, as well as law enforcement. We do understand that discovering our presence could be unsettling. We are willing and wanting to sit down with your government to hammer out the details how things will evolve from here and moving forward. Understand this…we've ruled ourselves for centuries and insist on being autonomous. We won't bend. We won't break. Leave us in peace, and we shall return in kind. There will be those who try to cause problems between humans and non-humans. We, the good people of the planet, cannot allow this. Don't let fear push you into violence. It seems to be the way of your people, but I implore you, don't let fear rule you. As we have indicated, we've always been here. Nothing has changed except that now you know…for certain. I'm done."*

The abrupt end to his speech gave Mary a chance to talk. She bounced in her chair as if she might burst if she didn't get to say something soon. *"I just want to say that I've been watching a lot of your television lately and I wanted to reach out to all of the little humans. Look at me. Look at how small I am. All my people are small and we can do anything! You can do anything too. Believe in yourself."*

Theron chuckled as the camera turned to him. When he stared at it, the interviewer cleared his throat. *"Any words?"*

"How do I follow that up?"

"Ha, ha, yes, that was a very nice little speech. You're quite the looker, all of you are. Is it normal for supernaturals to have superhuman beauty?"

Theron leaned back in his chair, crossed his legs at the ankle and tucked his thumbs in his belt loops. *"That and we're excellent lovers."* As cliché as he could be, the Centaur winked into the camera.

"I could throw up," Nala joked.

Colin spoke softly, his brow furrowed. "We're officially out of hiding." Everyone in the room looked at each other.

Nala felt Colin's worry, which mirrored her own emotions. She could only surmise the others in the room felt the same.

"Look, FOSE is on top of it. We knew this was coming. I'm surprised it took this long."

Tom leaned his fists on the table, edging toward her. "Did you know they were recording you in the café?"

A smile spread across her lips. "I was counting on it."

His brows shot toward his hair line. "Very well then."

"Look, Dr. Maryann said no more shifting until the pup is out. So I need to go for a walk. Jake, Tom, Tracy, can I count on you to spread the word throughout the pack? Everyone needs to be on their toes and on their best behavior when out in public. No one goes into town alone...at least two at a time, preferably more until we see how the humans react." She stood from the table and ran her hands over her swollen belly.

Colin's phone rang. He waved her on to go for her walk, apparently knowing she had to visit the lady's room...again...before her walk.

Finally outside, she spotted him approaching. "We can talk, but you'd better be prepared for a long walk," she warned, a smile planted on her lips. "I never imagined I'd be so restless."

"That call was Roman," he kissed her forehead, "and of course I'll walk with you."

She loved that her mate would walk with her every time. She enjoyed the walk not just to stretch her legs, but for the quiet time it gave them away from the pack.

"Xander has made a full recovery. Roman and Grace said it took a long time because he couldn't shift to heal. Something about brain damage. Anyway, Michelle sat with him the whole time and she's out for blood now that she can leave his side."

"Great," she whined. "Can't she just let FOSE handle it?"

"Would you, if it were our child?"

"Fair point." She stroked her belly. No, she couldn't just let FOSE handle it either. But she was tired of the bloodshed. Grace's plan was supposed to bring them to a time of peace.

"It will," Colin reassured her, having read her mind.

FIFTEEN

Summoned to the school once again, Nala was to bring her Beta. She was nervous to go back since her first two visits had ended in such violence.

Colin, unwilling to let his very pregnant mate out of his sight, insisted on going with. Tracy, for the first time since leaving Scottsboro had been left in charge.

Beauregard entered the conference room, interrupting pregnancy updates from Nala to Wendy and Grace. Ella was on his heel nearly dancing as she entered the room. They took their seats.

"I'll make this quick," he said. "Stephany Kincade has retreated to Chicago for the time being. The Scottsboro pack has assured FOSE that they have no desire to issue another challenge to the Belfast pack. However, they're still under our radar."

"That's good. I don't trust them." Nala said.

"Get to the good stuff!" Ella smacked him.

"That was the good stuff," he scowled at her and flipped open a file. "We have a special forces division opened up and we'd like Jake to consider leading that division as Alpha of that pack."

Nala's heart fell to the floor. Jake had been such a great Beta and he was family. She couldn't ask him to stay and give up the chance at being the Alpha he was meant to be. She forced herself to smile at him. "It's a great position, Jake."

"Yeah, but..." he looked down at the folder, then back up to Beauregard.

"There's a hefty salary in it for you, an Alphaship, and the satisfaction of rescuing helpless shifters. Are you up for the challenge?"

Jake looked back at the Fae King, staring at the giant man. "How could I say no?" His gaze shifted to Nala. "I'm sorry."

After she choked back the tears, she leaned forward and touched his hand. "You have my blessing, Jake. Go, be fantastic."

Oh God. What if there is a challenge? What next?

"To the issue of a challenge, there will be no more no quarter challenges directive issued by FOSE. This was a key sticking point with the human government. They don't take kindly to killing, unless it's in one of their death chambers."

"Death chambers?" Nala gulped.

Ella rolled her eyes. "When one of them does something really horrible, they have a trial by their peers. If they're guilty, they get sentenced to death by injecting poison into their veins. But they used to be put in gas chambers or something."

Nala swallowed hard. Did they want to do that to her for killing Jackson Kincade?

"For now, they have agreed to let us govern ourselves. This means we have to press on hard and fast with regard to the Separatists. This is why we need Jake. He's a strong Lycan male, set to be an Alpha. He's quick on his feet and with his mind. His own family has been a target, so he's vested in the outcome here. That's why we called this meeting, to offer Jake the position, and of course, to let you know about Mrs. Kincade." Ella leaned in and grabbed Nala's hand. "If you need any extra security until the birth of your child, let us know."

"Thank you." What was that? Did she know something? Was there another threat, or did she see her as a vulnerable *female*?

"It's because we just took your beta. Relax." Wendy pushed her thoughts at Nala.

Beauregard slid the file to Jake. "Everything you need to know is in there. You'll need to be in Charlotte by Monday."

"North Carolina?" Nala squeaked. *That far? That soon?*

The Fae King stood from his chair, stretching his long legs. "That's where the Special Forces are headquartered, and the call center, and FOSE. We're splitting into two divisions—East Coast and West. We'll divide the country in two and go from there. It's a work in progress."

Deciding not to question the King further, Nala only bobbed her head in understanding. "Good luck."

"Come on," Grace jumped out of her chair, "I have snacks waiting in our apartment."

Colin burst into laughter. "Bribing my pregnant wife with food, eh?"

"And babies. Tiffany is watching the twins with Zoltar." Wendy clapped her hands.

Grace walked over to Nala and winked. "Care for a lift?"

Her feet throbbed and ached always now that her belly was so swollen. "I can't believe I'm saying this. Sure."

Grace shifted into her massive wolf and crouched down. Colin helped her mount the Queen.

"This is awkward."

Wendy let out a giggle. "I swear, if I couldn't have shifted, Zoltar would have had to carry me around on his back for the whole last month. I was just so tired."

No shifting until the baby was born…that rule was the hardest on her. Feeling vulnerable and grunting every time she put her shoes on stunk, but she could live with it. Her wolf, so elated that they were with child, lay dormant most days.

When they reached Grace's door, she lay on the floor so Nala could dismount with Colin's help. Feeling slightly humiliated, she just held onto his neck and let him drag her off Grace's back. As soon as she was clear, the air around Grace shimmered as she took human form.

"Let's eat!"

When Grace opened the door, Tiffany was chasing a wolf pup through the room and Zoltar was helping his son stand on wobbly colt legs.

"Good boy!" He was beaming.

Nala was led by Wendy to the back patio where a chaise lounge waited for her, so she could put her feet up. Jake brought a plate of fruit, cheese, and meat to her with a tall glass of tea.

"Thank you," she said as she took the plate and glass from him. "So, are you excited?"

"Mostly, I'm worried about you." Colin's half-brother had the same nervous tick, running his hand through his hair.

"Don't be. I have Colin and the whole pack to look out for me. Congratulations, Jake. This is a really big deal. I'm so proud of you." She shook her head and forced a serious look on her face. "But who is going to harass my mate now?"

He laughed and took a seat on the chair next to her. "I guess I'm in shock. I didn't see this coming."

"How could you?"

"Right? Uh, there's something I want to tell you, but I'm afraid it'll upset you." He leaned on his knees. "So if it does, just punch me or something. Okay?"

Every time I come to this school, something bad happens! Despite her thoughts, she gave him a weak smile. "I'm sure I can handle it, whatever it is."

He took a deep breath, puffed out his cheeks, and released it. "I got a glance at that file. A list of suspects was included in my packet and… Brittany Merrill, Xander's half-sister and Jagger Merrill's demon spawn is one of the suspected Separatists."

Jagger Merrill will haunt me into my grave. "Guess you'd better track her down then, huh? For me?"

"That's just it…I think that's why they chose me. My sister was attacked. My Alpha. The school my Queen put in motion. It's personal for me."

She could feel the stress rolling off of him. While this might have been a hell of a leap forward for him, it wasn't without its cost. "That's why you're perfect, Jake. The outcome matters to you, not just for the sake of us integrating, but for the sake of your family. Do me a favor though?" Reaching over, she placed her hand on his forearm. "Don't make this about revenge. Make this about justice. Your job, I mean. It's about justice. The rest of us are okay."

He nodded and set his jaw. "I swear."

"Good, now, I'm going to eat this and try to get out of here before the sky falls or something."

"Good idea. We need to get back so you can decide who will be your Beta. I'll have to call Susan and break the news too." He stood from his chair and headed back inside.

"Jake…"

When he turned to her, she held his gaze for a moment. "Don't forget that you always have a home with us…as long as I draw breath, you can be a member of our pack." Her voice cracked at the last word. He was her brother too, not just her second-in-command. She hadn't realized how much she'd grown to love him until the thought of him leaving hit her like a tidal wave.

"Oh, I'll be around." He shot her a sideways grin and stepped inside.

She turned to stare at the grass, absentmindedly chewing on an apple slice. When she killed Jagger, felt the life drain from his body, she felt a sense of relief, a sense of freedom. No longer would she be a slave, or so she thought. The memory of her life in Scottsboro haunted her and her

Scottsboro pack mates. None of them had courted in the time they'd been at Belfast. They'd looked to her and she'd been strong, yet…none of them were mated.

The damage Jagger left in his wake was foul. She didn't know how to help them move forward and realized they couldn't, not yet. Not so long as he was haunting them through his children, through those that would seek to minimize others.

'Lower Lycans.'

She had a wrong to right and there was no time like the present.

"I'm coming with you," Grace said as she stepped outside.

"God, I'd ask you to stay out of my head, but right now, I need help getting out of this chair!" Nala held her hand out. Grace used it to heave her to her feet.

"It will be you and I. Colin can't go."

"Good luck telling him that." Nala laughed. "I'm surprised he's not out here checking my pulse already."

Grace used her royal powers to order Colin home, which severely pissed him off. "You can't do that!"

"I can and I did. Nala and I have some business to attend to. Take Jake home. Don't tell anyone about Jake's new position until Nala returns home to talk to her candidate. We'll see you there."

"Sorry, Bro," Roman laughed, "she has spoken." He shrugged.

As soon as their car left, Wendy summoned Theron. When he entered the room, she smiled at him like she was handing him a gift. "Go with Grace and Nala. If anyone gets in the way, or puts up a fuss, take care of it."

He slapped his hands together. "With pleasure." His gaze twitched in Tiffany's direction.

Tiffany blushed.

Nala noticed.

* * * *

When they pulled into the drive to the Scottsboro property, Grace grabbed Nala's hand and held it. "Breathe."

Nala took a deep breath.

"Jagger's not here."

"No, he isn't."

"It's just dirt and trees." Grace squeezed her hand. "You're a badass Alpha who happens to be very pregnant with your mate's child. You have a royal with you and a Centaur that's got a lot of pent up aggression."

Confused, Nala looked back at Theron. "What's that about?"

He groaned. "Celibacy until I get the balls to date the woman of my dreams."

She snickered. "Just ask Tiffany out. She's dying for you to."

"I know, but every time I open my mouth to talk to her, I vomit words that don't make sense. Word vomit. I don't know what the hell is wrong with me." He shook his head and fisted his hands. It was a nice distraction from Nala who hadn't realized they'd pulled up to the cottage...*the* cottage.

Theron got out of the car first, and opened the door for Nala, offering her a helpful hand out of the seat.

"Stephany left," a young woman said.

"I'm not here for her," Nala announced holding her head high. "I'd very much like to see Richard and Trina."

A man in a suit exited the cottage. His black hair slicked back, hands in his pockets. "They're not here."

Grace's eyes blazed purple. "Now why would you lie to your queen?" When his mouth gaped, she growled. "Go get them."

He nodded to the young woman they spoke to first. She shifted and ran toward the back of the property. Turning back toward them, he walked slowly. "So, you're the woman who killed my Beta?"

"Yes, he challenged me. I had no choice as he called no quarter." She could feel the heat coming off Theron as he

155

stepped closer to her.

"My new Beta tells me it was a fair fight, one-on-one."

"What's your point?" Grace crossed her arms over her chest.

His shoulders rose and fell. "That's impressive. I don't know many females that have the sort of fight in them."

Richard and Trina came into view. Trina's hair was a matted mess and looked like it hadn't been washed in weeks. Her clothes were also dirty and torn. Richard looked slightly better, clean at least.

"I've come to check on you," Nala called. As they walked closer, she noticed the dark circles under Trina's eyes. Her fears seemed to have been founded.

"We're fine," Richard said, grabbing Trina's arm.

Nala waddled forward, narrowing her eyes at him. "She doesn't look fine. She looks horrible. Why aren't you bathed? What's going on?"

"Lower Lycans don't get the same amenities..." Thomas spoke.

"Excuse me?" Grace leered at him. "What the fuck is a Lower Lycan?"

He rolled his eyes. "Lower class. Poor. They have to work for what they want."

"That's it!" Nala screamed. "Come home this instant. This is quite enough. You can't tell me this is how you want to live." Her palms grew sweaty and her heart raced. This is exactly what she fought against.

"Please," Trina started to say, but squeaked when Richard squeezed her arm.

Grace took two large steps and was nose to nose with Richard. "Take your hand off her arm before I eat it."

He released her and stepped back.

"Trina, do you wish to return to Belfast?" Grace asked, keeping her eyes and jaw set on Richard.

"Please, please let me go home," she wailed.

"Get in the car," Nala spoke softly. "We'll take you home."

"If you leave," Richard warned, "I will abjure you."

Trina collapsed on the forest floor. Her mate had cut her deep with his words.

"You what?" The electricity in Grace's voice reverberated through the air. "To your mate, you would do that?"

"I'm not living with Gnomes. I'm not living with anything but Lycans, as it should be."

Nala looked at the devastated woman on her knees, wounded so horribly, she didn't look like she'd ever recover. She'd been through God knows what and her mate threatened to sever their bond. She'd lived like that...a slave to the will of another. A bond was to be something beautiful, something cherished, and he was using it as a weapon.

Grace backed away. "Have it your way." She walked over and knelt by Trina. Her eyes shone bright but her words were soft, sweet. "Trina, I hereby release the magical bond between you and Richard. You are free."

Trina stood from the ground and smiled through her tears.

Richard, however, crumbled to the ground as the bond severed.

"I don't understand." Trina looked to him, then to Grace.

"I am your queen. With that responsibility comes certain powers. He used your bond against you. I released you from the pull of that bond, freed you from your prison. He wanted the pain, not you. So he can live with it."

Nala would have jumped in the air and screamed in triumph if not for the weight of her baby holding her feet to the ground. "Let's go home."

Thomas looked as if he wanted to protest, but thought better of it.

Theron groaned at the realization that there would be no fight.

They loaded into the car and left for Belfast.

Nala opened her window for fresh air, since Trina's uncleanliness was more than her pregnant self could handle. After a few deep breaths, she turned to face Trina in the back seat. "I knew something wasn't right there. I'd hoped you would have come back on your own. Now I can see you didn't have a say in the matter. But am I to understand that you will accept the Gnomes in our pack? That you will protect them as you would any other pack mate?"

"Yes, yes I will. I will be happy to. They were so nice, it's just that Richard—he"

Nala held up her hand. "You don't have to speak his name again. We'll figure out accommodations for you tonight, and then tomorrow, we'll work on getting you back into your home. Okay?" She realized the woman left with nothing more than the torn clothes on her back. That would not do. She had her own cottage before she left.

Trina began to cry again.

"No!" Nala scorned. "Belfast women are strong. Lycan women are strong. No more tears. You aren't homeless. True, the house you used to have has been purchased, but Wendy's old cabin is empty. I'm sure we can make arrangements. Just…stay in the main house tonight. We'll get you a bath, some clothes, and something to eat. Get a solid night's sleep and tomorrow is a new day. Okay?"

She wiped her eyes, smearing dirt on her face. Theron shifted uncomfortably next to her.

"You should ask Trina for advice," Grace said, glancing in the rearview.

"What?" he asked.

Grace's lips tightened into a thin line as she tried to hide her smile. "I believe she's good at dating advice. She could help you with your speech problem."

Apparently Grace knew something Nala didn't because Trina and Theron carried on all the way home. It had been the perfect distraction. By the time they pulled into the drive, Trina's spirits were lifted and Theron had a new sense of purpose about him.

Tracy and Colin ran out to greet them. When Colin saw Tracy, the state she was in, his pace slowed. He looked at Nala, anger in his face quickly vanishing as understanding set in. "You, my dear mate, are smarter than I."

"I know." She grabbed his hand. Turning to Tracy she smiled. "Tracy, can you please have someone set Trina up inside with a room, a shower and some clothes? Then meet me in the conference room. No, wait, have Jake call a meeting." She really wanted to put her feet up, but didn't want to waste any time making her announcement.

Her fingers pulled red hair behind her ear as she shook off her confusion. "Yes, I will, uh, do those things. Are you okay?" She looked at Trina.

She bobbed her head. "I am now. Thank you."

A small commotion behind them caused Nala to turn around. A group of five Gnomes gathered, spotting Trina's return. She slowly walked over to them and fell to her knees. "Please forgive my past actions toward you."

Ninny, a Gnome elder hobbled forward and placed her hand on Trina's forehead. "Calm yourself child. We can begin again. I'm Ninny. Why don't you allow my daughters, Heffa and Layla, come to your room to work these knots out of your hair? They're so good you won't feel a thing." She slid her tiny palm to Trina's cheek.

She nodded and rose to her feet, following Tracy into the pack house.

"Richard?" Colin asked.

"Grace separated their bond. He decided to stay behind."

Theron had moved to the front seat and waved goodbye as he closed the door behind him. As they drove off, Nala saw the pack beginning to gather by the fire pit. "Time to make an announcement."

Nala took a seat on a bench and put her feet up as she waited for everyone to gather. Once all were accounted for she stood, with Colin's help. Jake stood next to her with a stone faced expression. He wasn't about to give anything away.

"Thank you all for gathering on such short notice. I promise to make it quick. Jake has been given a position with FOSE that will include an upgrade to Alpha. Let's give him a round of applause." She began clapping, and everyone followed suit. When the noise deadened, she continued. "This, clearly, leaves the position of Beta open. It was my intention, prior to merging with the Belfast pack, to make Tracy my Beta. I'd very much like to offer her the position now. Are there any objections?"

Tracy's mouth fell slack. She stared at Nala, disbelief painted on her face.

When there were no objections, Nala smiled. "Tracy, please stand next to me." As soon as her new Beta was at her side Nala opened her arms toward the sky. "May the gods bless you as my Beta, guide you, and give you the strength and wisdom to protect and serve your pack."

Cheers erupted.

"Fine choice," Jake said as he shook Tracy's hand. A great show of faith for the rest of the pack that warmed Nala's heart. He leaned in toward her ear. "That means you get my room when I move in a few days. Nicer digs!"

She pulled her shoulders back, standing a bit higher. Despite the subterfuge with the threatening notes, Tracy had been her closest friend and confidant. She was a fierce warrior at heart and Nala felt comfortable having Tracy at the helm while she was moving to the birthing phase of her pregnancy. New pups could really drain a mother and Nala could use all of the help she could get.

Exhausted, she retreated with Colin to their room. He propped her swollen ankles up on a pillow and began lightly massaging her feet.

"We've gone through more changes in just over a year than ever in my lifetime." He smiled. "And the biggest change will be here any day."

She rubbed her tight belly. "Yes, I think contractions have started. It's so hard to tell, my belly is rock hard all of the time."

"How far apart are they?" he asked.

"Long enough for you to rub the other foot." She wagged her toes in his face.

"Nala!"

She rolled her eyes. "I'm serious. I think that was the first one. Well, maybe the second. I'm so tired, it's hard to tell."

He leaped off the bed and started pacing around the room. "But, wait. There's something we have to do."

"Colin, there's nothing we have to do except get to Dr. Maryann by the time they are five minutes apart. It's my first child. This could take an entire day. Just calm down." She rolled to her side and watched him continue to pace.

"No, you don't understand. I've been keeping something from you. I have a big secret. I want to show you but you just put your feet up and now the baby is coming and…"

"Keeping what from me? Colin, you need to breathe."

"Think, think, think," he slapped his forehead with each word.

She heard his voice scream out in her head. *"Grace, I need you, immediately!"*

"Colin, what is going on?"

"No, oh no." He rushed to the edge of the bed and knelt down next to it, scooping her hand in his. "It's not bad. Rather it is a surprise. Just…trust me."

He helped her off the bed, down the stairs to the drive. They made it at the same time Grace was pulling back in the drive. When she jumped out of the car with concern in her eyes, Colin apologized. Before he could finish, she was grinning.

"Don't sweat it, I read your thoughts. You're doing an excellent job keeping Nala out of your head right now." She shifted into her wolf and crouched down.

"Your ride," Colin snickered as she pulled her hand toward Grace.

Mounted atop her queen for the second time, Colin shifted to wolf and led Grace down a path at the back of the property. The path came to an opening which contained a two story log cabin. A ribbon was tied to a beam on the porch.

"Colin?"

Once in human form, he was at Nala's side helping her off of Grace's back. "I had this built, while you've been preoccupied. It has four bedrooms, in case we decide to have more children."

Tears stung her eyes. She tried to blink them away. "Oh my God, it's beautiful." She grabbed her stomach and bent over as a contraction took hold. When it was over, she stood up and blew out a breath.

Colin and Grace exchanged excited smiles.

"Okay, you have to let me see it now." Grace elbowed Colin in the ribs.

Colin led them inside the front door. There was a stone fireplace in the living room, a dining room, a nice sized kitchen with a huge center island, a master suite, a nursery for the baby and two spare bedrooms, one of which had been made into an office.

Nala rubbed her belly and leaned against the door jamb of the nursery. "Shit, that hurts."

Grace's eyes began to glow their royal glow.

"Something wrong?" Nala asked, looking at her clearly feeling some sort of emotion.

"I'm ready to have pups too. We are just waiting for the next heat." With a soft smile, she blinked a few times until her eyes went back to normal. "Anyway, that was the second contraction in six minutes. Why don't you let me give you a lift to Dr. MaryAnn?"

Sixteen

With her new baby boy in her arms, Nala sobbed tears of gratitude. "He's so beautiful."

"Do we have a name?" Dr. MaryAnn asked.

Colin kissed her forehead. "Chase, because that's all we're going to do for the next few years is chase him around."

She'd already picked Benjamin as a name. Perhaps it would wait for her next child. "Chase, I like that name." She stroked the sleeping infant's cheek. She could not believe her eyes. Once fearful she'd get pregnant with a baby against her will, her desire to never create life had been usurped by a strong desire to start a family with Colin. She'd been blessed with a new life and knew how completely rare that was.

"Care for a visitor?" Jake poked his head in the room.

"Come on in!" Colin threw his arm around his brother's shoulder. "Meet your nephew, Chase."

Jake had a stuffed wolf for the baby and a box of candy for Nala. "There are tons of gifts in your cabin. Gustav and Michelle are there now, baby-proofing the place.

Weird, the thought of a vampire baby-proofing anything. But Michelle had brought about a new sense of humanity in him. The undead man seemed alive around her, and she at peace when she was with him.

"Well, Gustav is doing his teleporting thing, bringing gifts from everyone at the college while Michelle baby-proofs. Whatever, they're working on it." Jake sat on the edge of the bed. "I'm so happy for the two of you."

"Would you like to hold him?" Nala offered.

He froze for a moment before slowly nodding. "How do I do it without hurting him? He's so tiny."

Nala instructed him on supporting the baby's head and eased Chase into his uncle's arms.

"Wow, he's no bigger than my boot!" Jake rocked slightly while holding Chase in his arms. "This really gives me the motivation to excel at my new job. We have to make a better, safer world for him." He looked to Colin. "I trust you can handle things without me here?"

"How will I ever manage without your constant harassment?" He crossed his arms over his chest, a permanent smile frozen to his face.

"Right? I'm going to have to delegate those duties."

Tracy came into the room with the scanner to grab Chase's foot print. "Oh he's so precious!" She squealed. She scanned his foot, and then placed the scanner on the bed, scooping the baby out of Jake's arms.

"Guess I'm done with the kid...for now." He looked at Colin and wagged his brow. "Until he's old enough to corrupt."

"When I'm done holding the baby, the doc said they can go home." Tracy kissed his forehead. "But I'm not done yet."

Home. Home sounded good. She wanted to put the baby to bed and take a nice hot shower.

"Oh my goodness Nala, look what you did! He's just amazing." She cooed at the baby who continued to sleep.

Colin playfully threw his hands on his hips. "Hey, I had

something to do with it too."

"Okay. Mom's ready to go home. Put the baby in the bassinet and let the doctor know I'm ready." Nala was done with visits. She was more than ready to be in her new home, with her mate and new baby alone.

Before she could clear the room Roman and Grace entered, ushering everyone else out and together, they blessed Chase. As they held hands and said the blessing, Nala could swear she felt the room buzzing. Whatever juice they had was real enough.

* * * *

Finally in her new home, she put the baby to bed and took a nice, hot shower. Colin made a tray of snacks for her and had it waiting in the living room by the fire. She eased herself onto the blankets he'd placed by the fireplace and grabbed up a hunk of cheese.

They sat quietly watching the flames dance. She could feel waves of emotion coming from him, feelings of love, elation, and pure awe at their son.

"He's so spectacular, Nala. Thank you."

"Thank me? For what?"

"For giving me a son, a family, for giving me love again. I never thought...I just..."

"Never thought you'd recuperate from losing your mate and your child?" She spoke for him, words clearly evading him, or was it fear of dampening the mood?

"Yes. That."

"It's okay, Colin. I'm in disbelief too. I'm so thankful because I never thought I'd have any of this. You, Chase, this home, this pack. It just seems so unreal, especially when I think about where I was two years ago." She took a deep breath and let it go. "We can't hide from the past. We may not have to relive it constantly, but it's made us who we are today. I can't speak for you, but the horror of my past is exactly what makes me appreciate what I have today."

Stretching out his fingers, he brushed a stray hair behind her ear. "You are absolutely right."

"But the truth is, you'll never forget your first mate. I will never forget Jagger, especially with his spawn out there wreaking havoc. FOSE still hasn't tracked down the Separatists. We might be safer, but we still have to be vigilant. The hauntings of our past only make us stronger in that regard. We know how to be on guard."

Her words reverberated through them both. Chase was their primary concern now. Nala still had to head the pack, but the safety and security of their child was their foremost concern…and they had Jake out there making them safer.

He kissed her cheek and pushed off the floor getting to his feet. "I'll be back."

Confused why he was headed outside she asked where he was going.

"I have to pee and Michelle put some kind of crazy locks on the toilet!"

She laughed. Yes, they certainly had new concerns.

THE END

OTHER BOOKS BY ANITA COX

Interested in learning how Grace came to the Belfast pack? You can find out in the Prequel, Pursuing Grace, which is free on Amazon, All Romance, Kobo and Google Play. If you don't have accounts at those retailers, you can download a copy straight from the author's website at http://authoranitacox.com on the Books tab.

Dirty White Candy Series
The Beginning, Book 1
Ultimate Vacation, Book 2
Trading Places, Book 3

Shifter Chronicles
Pursuing Grace, Prequel
Saving Grace, Book 1
Resurrection, Book 2
No Quarter, Book 3

Tales of the Asgard
Valkyrie

About Anita

Anita Cox is a bestselling author of a growing number of novels. For over ten years, she's written contemporary, erotic, and paranormal, romances via traditional, independent, and audio publishers.

An only child born and raised in the Midwest, Anita enjoyed reading novels as a way to occupy herself and set her imagination free. That propensity blossomed into creations of her own as she began crafting novels. As she matured, she began writing more adult tales and donned the penname Anita Cox.

Anita resides in Indiana with the last teenager in her herd, a fluffy-not-fat cat named Tommy Chong, Titan the English Mastiff and the husband that helped create her creative penname. In her free time, Anita enjoys fishing, gardening, and devouring equal portions of strong coffee and well-written novels.